The
Last
Days
of My
Mother

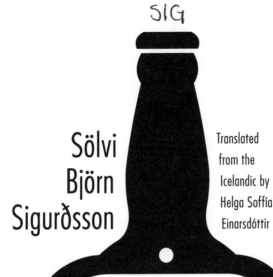

Sölvi
Björn
Sigurðsson

Translated
from the
Icelandic by
Helga Soffía
Einarsdóttir

The
Last
Days
of My
Mother

OPEN LETTER
LITERARY TRANSLATIONS FROM THE UNIVERSITY OF ROCHESTER

Library of Congress Cataloging-in-Publication Data: Available upon request.
ISBN-13: 978-1-934824-73-3 / ISBN-10: 1-934824-73-9

This project is supported in part by an award from
the National Endowment for the Arts.

ART WORKS.
arts.gov

Translation of this novel was made possible thanks to the support of
Bókmenntasjóður - the Icelandic Literature Fund.

Bókmenntasjóður
The Icelandic Literature Fund

Printed on acid-free paper in the United States of America.

Text set in Dante, a mid-20th-century book typeface designed by Giovanni Mardersteig.
The original type was cut by Charles Malin.

Design by N. J. Furl
Cover art incorporates: Intravenous Drip by Emily Haasch from The Noun Project

Open Letter is the University of Rochester's nonprofit, literary translation press:

The
Last
Days
of My
Mother

Chapter
1

I had decided to take Mother to die in Amsterdam. The terminal echoed the discords of the northern gales outside, and behind us herds of drowsy people trudged along toward the security gates. Mother stood next to me in silent conversation with the cosmos while rummaging through her handbag. She believed in maximum utilization of carry-on luggage and made sure I carried my weight—and hers. I'd suggested sending a box or two by mail or paying for the extra weight, but she wouldn't hear of it. It was simply *depressing* to watch how I squandered money.

"Like that apartment you shared with Zola," she continued while we fed our things onto the conveyor belt for the X-ray machine. "Very high maintenance, that woman. And then she just takes off with some Frenchman."

"That's not quite what happened."

"Mind you, you're much better off without her, Trooper. I know you don't like to talk about it, but let me just say this once and for all: she didn't deserve you."

Mother walked through the security gate and was stopped by a young woman in uniform who ran a metal detector up and down her body. "Anything in your pockets? Belt?"

Like always, when astonished by something in my presence, Mother turned around and stared at me.

"Just take off the belt and go through again," I said.

"What nonsense. I suppose I should take of my shoes, too?"

"Well, yes, since I see you have a metal heel," the woman said.

"I've never met anyone so rude in my life. And I've been all over."

"It's standard procedure. Heightened security after 9-11."

"Nine-eleven? Do we all speak American now? Do you mean November 9th?"

"Mother."

"No, I mean it. First you're asked to strip and then you're ordered around in gibberish."

"Let's just get this over with."

Cursing under her breath, Mother walked through. The officer turned to me with a tiny pot of hair gel that I'd recently bought for a small fortune.

"I'm afraid I can't let you take this on board."

I sighed, snatched the jar out of her hands, scooped out the contents and smeared it into my hair.

"Hah!" Mother roared with laughter. "Look at you, Trooper! *Quelle coiffeur!* It defies gravity. Excellent!"

I was about to crack a joke about exploding hair gel but managed to bite my tongue. There was no way of knowing what Mother might do if this dragged on any longer.

"*Mein Gott!*" she groaned as we headed into the passenger lounge. "Finally, Trooper, we're on our way! Well, I think we deserve to sit down and have a proper drink. How about it, Trooper? *Ein Schnapps?*"

★

4

My life hadn't always been like this. Just a few months earlier I had been living with a woman who'd have sex with me with the lights on and found comfort in a double bed and a dishwasher, still confident that the future would roll out at least a slightly discolored red carpet. But Fortune turned her back on me. Love kicked me in the balls. Over the course of a single disastrous week in January, a seven-year relationship went down the drain. I found myself lying stark naked in a hotel room in Dublin, blinded by toxic levels of alcohol and in total ignorance of who lay next to me. My intoxication was such that I had difficulty discerning the gender of the person and didn't realize until I was alone again that whoever it was had been sexually stimulated by beating me with a stuffed animal. The experience was unpleasant, but necessary for my personal growth. I was slowly coming to understand that the various doubts I'd harbored about my relationship had been based on misunderstanding. I had squandered my happiness. The lesson was terrible and all I could do was head back home.

The dreary spring of 2008 hung over Iceland like rotten debris from the murky depths of history, threatening financial devastation, sleep deprivation. And then Mother was diagnosed with cancer.

I had accompanied her to the hospital, less than a month before we embarked on our journey. She wore a red, fitted wool two-piece, as if she believed that the better she looked the harder it would be for the doctor to deliver bad news with conviction. A woman who looked this chic at her age could hardly be at death's door.

The doctor, however, was grave. He held a pen up to his chin and gave the desk a small tap before he spoke. The test results were back and as we could see on the X-rays, the gray area on the shinbone was growing. "We believe that what we have here is sarcoma of the connective tissue." Mother gave the doctor a cold stare and waited for him to expand on the subject. "Fibrosarcosis is one type of osteocarcinoma, which is, in fact, rather rare in patients your age. We do see it in other mammals, cats and dogs in particular, but it's extremely rare to diagnose this disease so late in life."

"Really now. And is there a prize?" Mother asked.

"Pardon me?"

"No. Spare me the circus act, Herr Doctor. You tell me I have a disease only found in children and pets as if I'd won the lottery. It's absurd!"

Mother's impatience was palpable. She would grumble about the medical corps being comprised of sadists who flocked to medical school fascinated by stories of Mengele's ghoulish experiments. To her the nurses were variations of Herta Oberhauser, a Nazi nurse who murdered her victims by injecting them with kerosene. Mother had played Herta in a controversial play in a small Montparnasse theatre and knew what she was talking about. I ignored these rants. After all, the sentiment was not a recent development. Mother had suffered from a phobia of hospitals for as long as I could remember, and made several efforts to cultivate in me a similar distrust of the medical profession. It was wiser, she thought, to follow the example of Great Aunt Edda when you were under the weather: have a little drink to ease the pain, and then another just for luck. I pointed out that strong spirits were hardly a cure for cancer and that she had to be a bit more understanding of the hospital staff. And I suppose she tried, even though she failed fantastically.

"Maybe I should have gone to the vet, Herr Doctor?"

"No, no, not at all, Mrs. Briem," the doctor stammered. "Cell division in people your age is not very rapid, which means that the disease spreads more slowly."

"Right. And so you will, of course, fix this before that happens."

"Well," the doctor began, breaking into a long speech about matters being slightly more complicated. There certainly were cases where doctors had managed to surgically remove sarcoma from connective tissue, but a very large team of specialists was needed for such an operation. Unfortunately, Icelandic hospitals had neither the equipment, nor the manpower for such an undertaking. The operation would have to take place in the United States, but since the procedure was still experimental, it would not fall under the Icelandic Health Care System. Mother would have to pay for it herself.

"There is, however, quite a good chance of getting sponsors for semi-profiled operations of this magnitude. Surgeons may waive their fees, research institutes invest in the operations in exchange for exclusive rights to acquired information."

"Ok, alright," I said, my hopes already up. "And how do we do this?"

"I can look into it, make a few inquiries. The fact that this is such a rare case should work in our favor."

"I don't understand where you're going with this," Mother said. "Do you think I'm some kind of guinea pig? We both know perfectly well that no one is going to pay for this operation. I'm not a celebrity. And what company will put up a fortune for an old hag from Iceland?"

I'd never heard Mother refer to herself as old, and certainly never as a hag, but this seemed to achieve the desired effect: the doctor was suddenly at a loss for words. He stared blankly at her and fiddled with his pen.

"See, I thought that a doctor's job was to help patients," Mother continued, "not to breed false hopes of some American Utopia."

"If we pay for this ourselves," I interjected, ". . . do you have any idea what that would add up to?"

The doctor cited some astronomical number that was beyond my comprehension. What I did comprehend was that, even if we sold the apartment, withdrew all my savings, sold every internal organ I could spare and the rest of me off into slavery, it wouldn't even make a dent in the costs.

"It's not worth it, Trooper. All this for a shot in the dark? No."

"As I was saying, this is the most promising option you have," the doctor mumbled, "but there are alternatives. One is to do nothing: your life expectancy is three to six months. Twelve with chemo. Another is to amputate. That could buy you five years, and with chemo before and after we could . . ."

"You're not taking my leg."

"Mother . . ."

"Out of the question. I'm sixty-three years old and I've had this leg all my life. Nothing changes that."

"This is a matter of life and death."

"Well, then I'll just die!"

She leaned forward in her chair and burst into tears. It was unbearable.

"We'll fight this," I finally managed to say. "We'll do everything we can."

"Take off my leg? Pump me so full of chemicals that I won't be able to eat? Just so that I can make it to seventy and invite the leftover, half-dead scarecrows to some pathetic birthday party at the Freemason's Hall? I'm dying, Trooper. It was always a matter of time."

She stood up and walked out of the room. The doctor handed me a calling card with an emergency number and told me to be in touch as soon as we decided on how we wanted to proceed. We took a taxi back home. Mother went straight to her bedroom and left me alone in the living room, surrounded by a silence impregnated with years of memories.

I had grown up in this apartment, left home and returned again well into my thirties with my tail between my legs to hide away once more in the attic. The inflation of my body over the past few months provided a strong argument for those who believe that obesity is a growing social problem. In the mornings I'd stand naked, gawking at myself in a full-length mirror. My bloated body resembled a fisherman wearing a flesh-toned parka over neoprene waders. I blamed glandular hyperactivity, but deep down I knew that the real culprits were the bakery across the street and the sherry-marathons Mother and I regularly indulged in. It had been four months since Zola left me to shack up with that French dentist and his lantern jaw. Since then my life had been devoid of substance. I lived in a world limited by the seams of my pajamas. The diminutive nature of this world was confined to even less significant acts like fly-tying and online car racing. In the evenings I'd come down and have a drink with Mother—her own home brew, which she claimed was better than any wine sold in the liquor store. Almost every aspect of my body and personality surrendered to the law of gravity. My face was bloated and the rest of me was somehow rubbery, as if I were one big tennis elbow, from head to toe. There was nothing to suggest, as I had claimed when I first moved in, that my stay in the attic was a temporary arrangement until I found a flat for myself. I came into Mother's life like a stand-in for the company she craved, and we'd grown used to this little by little; spending our days drinking sherry and reading tarot cards while I continued to tell myself: Tomorrow I'll get going, tomorrow I'll get off my fat ass and start a new life.

But it wasn't until that day, the day Mother was told that she was dying, that I faced reality. I walked around studying the apartment in a trance, lightheaded from the inevitability of impermanence. Each nook and cranny became a tunnel to the past. Freud in dust form. A biography of molecules. My life floated by and suddenly I was overcome by relief—this was not the end of everything, but a new beginning. Time itself, that mismatched resin of shapeless days and self-pity, became an unbroken, unwavering and crystal-clear image before my very eyes. From now on, each day would be a work of art and the brushstrokes governed by this one goal: to make Mother happy during the last days of her life.

I was filled with such exuberance that I laughed out loud, as if nothing had ever pleased me as much as Mother's imminent death. I ate a pepperoni stick and poured sherry into a tall glass of Coca-Cola, surfed aimlessly on the Internet like a bar-hopping drunk until I finally found a website on "Ukrain," a miracle drug developed by Dr. Wassyl Nowicky. The reports were astounding. A Danish man, who had spent weeks rotting away in a semi-coma, deserted by friends and family, had recovered fully thanks to this treatment and even won a regional marathon a few months later.

Was this the answer?

Dr. Nowicky had developed the drug from greater celandine extract. The formula was created in Ukrainian research labs during the Cold War, and then developed further in Austria, the alchemist's current country of residence. He had struggled for decades to get the drug registered but fate was against him. The authorities spat on him. Hounded by both an Israeli terrorist organization and the CIA, Nowicky stood alone, out on the margins with his flower. Inevitably he associated himself with the left-wing, which would no doubt work in my favor when trying to convince Mother to take Ukrain. She hated Conservatives more than death.

As I sat in front of the computer knocking back sherry, a blanket of calm settled over my soul. I was slightly intimidated by the idea of taking Mother to some former Soviet country, but they seemed to be the only ones with a formal license to use Ukrain as a treatment for cancer. I pictured vodka parties in the Carpathian Mountains, fat mustachioed men in caviar baths after a long night of drinking, and Mother nostalgically exchanging dollars on the street for local currency. She had travelled to Eastern Europe in the '80s to feed her spirit, as she called it, *for the soul still had value in the Old Soviet.* "Unlike the States," she went on, "with all its consumerism and shareholders. No, Trooper, I'd rather drink water with Comrade Boris." She was referring to a severe hangover in Moscow when they had all run out of alcohol and had to make do with water.

Even though Mother's pseudo-communism had diluted with age, I wasn't sure I could handle a replay of her "Eastern Adventures" and felt relieved when I read that some institutes in the West had started offering Ukrain treatment: The Holiterapias Institute in Lisbon, Dove House in Hampshire, Pro-Leben Clinic in Vienna. There was not much information, aside from a link for a treatment clinic in the Netherlands called Libertas. I clicked on this and waited while a photograph of an old mansion appeared on the screen. In front of the building, a few people stood in a semi-circle with the chief physician, Dr. Frederik, in the middle. Above his head was a speech bubble saying: "Welcome to Lowland, where we have been treating individuals since 1963."

Libertas seemed to be both a treatment center and a hospice. People came to die at Lowland, but also to hope for a last chance at recovery: "Our decades of experience in treating patients with advanced cancer and the sensitive work of palliative treatment makes Libertas a viable choice in difficult circumstances." The more I read the more I felt this was the right choice for Mother. Dr. Nowicky's magic drug seemed likely to increase her odds considerably, and most importantly—nobody was denied available drugs for easing pain and suffering. "People who are alive are not dead," the site claimed. "And life is the basis of our foundation."

Morphine, Ukrain, Ecstasy . . . in my mind's eye I saw Mother not only fit and strong, but cruising the racetracks of happiness. "I've got it!" I exclaimed, bursting into her room. "We'll go to the Netherlands!"

"What are you talking about?"

"We'll go to Libertas and meet with Dr. Frederik."

The light in the room deepened and faded away with each word Mother didn't say, and my belief in the perfect solution choked on her silence. Nearly all her life she had lived with an unpleasant fascination with death, but now, when a thorough examination of her bone marrow confirmed that it was finally time, it was as if she'd never heard that people could actually die. She was in shock.

"It's not as if I haven't been dying all along," she finally said and whimpered a little because all of this started as the tiniest tickle in her belly in Berlin, the night I first made myself known and Willy Nellyson ran off to Italy. "And there I was all alone, Trooper, and then I had you."

"So the story goes."

"It's no story, Hermann, these are stone cold facts. Why did he just up and leave like that? Didn't even leave a note."

"I don't know, but about this clinic—"

"And me, there, all alone in Germany. Look how beautiful he was, tall like a prince and sharp as a sword."

She handed me the photograph of Willy Nellyson and I remembered why I'd always doubted that this man was my father. Such a paternity claim was as absurd as two weeks of abstinence on Spítala Street. If my looks were a work of fiction, the outcome would be *War and Peace* or some other endless novel, bulky and thick yet strangely lacking in mass. A paperback. Willy Nellyson, however, was a tall, willowy man with a few stray hairs growing out of his chin, reminiscent of some sort of academic catfish, so peculiarly hunched that he seemed to have had his bones removed, perhaps during the war, so that he could be conveniently folded into a carry-on bag. He had betrayed Mother by running off after I was conceived and, according to her—this was something she said over and again—something within her died after his getaway, something she never got back, scarring her for life. Her epic death flowed like a branching river through my childhood, in different versions that all confirmed the same thing: men were a dubious species poisoning the lives of striking women. Only one thing distinguished Willy Nellyson: he had the perfect cock. This I deduced from a carved ebony dildo Mother kept on the top shelf of the living room cupboard, and which she'd taken down on my thirteenth birthday, handed it over with gusto and said: "This, Trooper, is your father's penis." I fondled the wood as if it held promises of a great future and waited, for years and without reward, for my father's heritage to manifest itself between my legs.

"How strange a lifetime is. Over sixty years and then . . ."

She looked defeated. I retreated out of the room and started to ramble dead drunk around the apartment, my mind wandering aimlessly, to Dublin, Moscow, and the distant features of Zola. The next morning I woke up hung over; Ukrain and Libertas only scattered images in a saturated mind. Mother? Dying? Amsterdam? The silence of the room grew in proportion with the stench of my bed sheets and for three, four—perhaps five—days, depression inhabited Spítala Street.

But as Mother said every so often: One week is Yang and the other Yin. Sometimes you just need time to put things in perspective. I had almost given up on the idea of the Netherlands when I saw a TV report on how *lively* Amsterdam was. Bit by bit things started to look up again. I contacted Libertas and received brochures with information and rates, spent my savings on a five-star hotel in Amsterdam, and finally sat down with Mother to discuss things. It took a few days to explain to her what this trip really entailed; leaving Iceland once and for all—the final journey. Her heartbreak was unbridled for a couple days, but then she composed herself. On Saturday evening she appeared in the attic, a bottle of sherry in hand, and told me that she'd browsed through the brochures. The lightness that had engulfed me that first night made a cautious comeback with a touch of grounded strategy. Great expectations swarmed beneath the surface.

"I got out my cards and let them decide. I don't expect to recover, Trooper. I've come to terms with the inevitable. The end is near, but not here yet. I've never seen cards like this before. Do you think that your dreams can come true, even moments before you die?"

I squeezed her hand and the next morning I confirmed our booking with Libertas. The following days were spent preparing for departure. Now we stood groggy in the airport terminal rubbing the last remnants of sleep from our eyes. For a second I tried to imagine what lay in store for us on the other side of the ocean, but the thought flew away before I could catch it.

Chapter
2

"Ahhh," Mother sighed, walking into the Duty Free area, as if she'd just repeated the Feat of the Long Walk to the Irish pub on her fiftieth birthday. I was becoming increasingly depressed by how much everything had changed since I was last here. The Duty Free store had been moved to another part of the building, I wasn't going away to Ireland with Zola. My face drooped involuntarily, stunned by the ruthlessness of the separation.

I was still at the mercy of such fits of melancholy. The slightest reminder of Zola had similar effects as cannabis poisoning: I'd grow pale and become inconsolable without the omnipresence of high-calorie snacks. Remembering Zola's obsession with ballet and folk music did nothing to ease the pain. For seven blissful years she'd filled my life with a buoyancy that transported me from one place to another, without the anguish and defeat that usually defined my existence. She was relentlessly horny, like a fly that only has a single day to procreate, and she made me try all sorts of things I had little to no knowledge of beforehand.

My fascination with her body didn't fade, even though she suddenly had enough one day, diverting her impulses and appetites instead toward confectionaries, dismissing me as a graduate from the university of love. The fun and games were over. We'd have sex on a monthly basis, going through the motions out of duty or to avoid a bulletproof reason for going our separate ways. I'd see the female form everywhere, in the most mundane things, like a toothbrush, but Zola was lost to me. It never crossed my mind that these were symptoms of a dying love, that I would stumble naked around hotel rooms where some of the most meaningless sex acts in the world were performed with my involvement. What followed were attacks of self-pity, overeating, and intensive staring into refilled sherry bottles during the months I moved back into Mother's attic.

"Hermann!" Mother shook me as I stood shuddering in the camera department. "Are you lost in space?"

"Yes. Well. No."

"I'm going to have a drink at the bar. Knowing you, you'll be here for a while spending money on junk."

We parted ways and I wandered around the camera section where a tanned couple straight out of a magazine glided between the shelves. The boy looked like a professional athlete and the girl like Miss California, lean and blonde with endless legs. Their appeal was so conventional that they could have been off-the-rack, like her short denim dress. I almost bumped into them when she suddenly charged and snaked her body around the boy's, who reacted like a defense basketball player to swiftly secure a position for them between the Samsungs and the Sonys to swap spit. I was relieved when the whiff of animal fat seduced me into the Food Market, where I bought gum and a newspaper, then filled out a questionnaire on Icelandic lamb. I did this in part to make up for Mother's loathing of any and all surveys, which she regarded as an evil of capitalism and mass surveillance. When I found her at the bar she was staring into the mirror, sporting huge sunglasses.

"Strange how I was never a dean's wife," she said, blowing cosmopolitan smoke rings at her reflection. "Why has my love life always been so . . . ? Take Jonas for example. It's not my fault that the man was so sickly all the time."

"I ran into him in the bakery the other day and he seems to be doing better, he's walking again—"

"It was hopeless," she injected and stubbed out her cigarette. "A man who's in rehab when he's not actually in the hospital? No. What I've never had, Trooper, is a man who could support me. Look at those two over there. It's obvious what they've been up to."

"What do you mean?"

"Obviously homosexuals."

"Ah, but of course! I *was* wondering what's up with their asses," I said, ignoring the disapproving looks from the people on the next table. Truth was, Mother had a real soft spot for gay men.

"Why on earth do all the best men go into this? No wonder women my age have trouble finding a man."

"Oh, for crying out loud, Eva."

"No, I mean it. Either they're married to some *sad cow* or feeling each other up. Can you name one normal, single man my age?"

I reached for my Food Market bag and pretended to read the celebrity pages of my newspaper. The main story was about Croatian supermodels Milla and Iva.

"Although . . . you know . . . I always thought you'd turn out gay, Trooper," she continued. "I've never known any child as dramatic as you were. You'd dress up in my clothes, put on makeup, walk around in over-sized heels . . ."

"You raised me in the theater, what did you expect?"

17

"Sure, but just think, a beautiful woman like me—surrounded by homosexuals her whole life. Then along come these old farts like Emma Gulla . . . apparently she bagged herself a doctor."

"Who's Emma Gulla?"

"Don't you remember her? Such an incredibly ugly woman. And boring, too."

A nearby screen announced that our flight was boarding. I picked up our things and prepared to go.

"Wait. Let's have one for the road, Trooper."

"We'll miss our flight."

"I doubt they'll take off without us."

"Eva," I sighed.

"Alright, alright. I've got a little something with me anyways."

We walked along the seemingly endless corridor toward the gate. Mother was astonished at the lack of moving sidewalks and gave the flight attendant a long speech about the technological superiority of German airports. The Samsung-girl in the short denim dress sat in the seat across the aisle from me.

"Isn't that the same dress I gave Zola?" Mother whispered, but I was too overwhelmed by the girl's presence to answer. She fastened her seatbelt while her boyfriend wrestled with his laptop, giving me a chance to stare at her legs and wonder how some human of the male sex, some sweaty, hick ape had actually been a part of her conception. I'd much rather believe that the Samsung-girl was the fruit of intense sex between the supermodels Milla and Iva. Mother, however, repeated her suspicions of the girl's mundane part in the material world, took a swig from her flask and said: "Yes, I'm sure that's the same dress."

"What dress are you talking about?"

"Well, that *dress* I gave Zola. She made it into this huge issue, remember? She could be so incredibly opinionated."

I remembered. A couple years earlier Mother had held a gala on Palm Sunday, inviting pensioners, neighbors, and distant relatives who had the required weakness for wine. The day before the party Mother had stopped by with a dress she'd bought on a whim for Zola during a shopping frenzy at the mall's end-of-season sale. Zola didn't like showing too much skin and was horrified by the short hemline. Mother insisted she wear it and then made an alcohol-induced presentation of Zola in the dress, parading her about the party, to show off what a fantastic stylist she was, the gorgeousness of the dress, how great Zola looked in it, and how wonderful the whole thing was. The tension escalated as the evening progressed, something detonated between them; there was shouting and crying and we left without good-byes. Zola said she'd had it and demanded that I talk to Mother or she'd never step foot in that house again. The next morning I took a taxi down to Spítala Street. Mother came to the door and welcomed me in high spirits. Now we'd have a fun hangover day! But instead of sharing a drink with her, I brought up the incident.

"What?"

"Just, you know. You were being difficult. That speech, for instance, about Willy Nellyson and his cock."

"That was just a joke."

"And then you asked Zola if I was any good."

"Really? In bed?"

"That was the only way to interpret it."

"Oh. And what did she say?"

"That's beside the point. You need to learn to behave in company."

She asked if this was a message from Zola and I told her to knock it off, that she knew very well that this wasn't about Zola.

"Well, I don't remember you speaking to me like this before you met that woman."

"*That woman.* Is that how you think of her? The woman who took days off work to . . ."

"Oh, Trooper, let's not bring that up."

"By all means, let's. I want to know what you mean."

"Well, nothing really. I just don't recall you making a habit of attacking people before this relationship."

"I'm not attacking anyone. You were the one who . . ."

"Know what, Trooper? There's no point in this. I worry about you, that's all. You're so terribly codependent."

After this I was stuck for a while in no man's land between the two women, like melted cheese between two slices of toast. I talked to Mother on the phone every now and then, but spent my days with Zola. I woke up next to her and cooked with her and in the evenings after we'd tidied up, I'd tell her stories from work about people who wanted to buy out their neighbors in order to build a sauna in the basement, and colleagues who bought dogs to go jogging with but ended up keeping them in a pet hotel while they themselves developed a high-maintenance cocaine addiction. Zola had no faith in my profession. She believed real estate agencies were the final indicator of the degeneration of modern man, the moral bankruptcy of capitalism, and the distorted image of people who stare into the bathroom mirror to define their lives, but perceive nothing but the tiles. I should quit and elope with her to Ireland.

"Ireland!?" Mother was practically foaming at the mouth.

"Just for a while. Zola's going to study geology."

"I'd think the best place for that would be *Iceland.*"

"We just want a change of scenery."

"Ahh . . . well, of course you do," she said in a calmer tone tainted with newfound excitement. "This will be great! I've got lots of frequent flyer miles."

In order to appease Zola I decided to enroll in a practical course in Dublin's Trinity College, settling on a diploma in Freudian Analysis. My first class was unlike anything I'd tried before. I became a spokesman for phenomenology, an advocate of idealism; dressed in striped shirts and tweed jackets that underlined my transformed status in human society. Fellow students envied my naïve passion for Sigmund and wondered at the intimate, personal relationship I formed with him. As I stared into my own essence, a whole new world of theory opened up like a blender for the miscellaneous gumbo of soul and psyche.

The guileless euphoria over my relationship with the psychoanalyst only lasted a couple of weeks, however. I realized that even though my Austrian friend had great insight into the human soul, his writings were lacking in practical solutions. I was left with a deep, almost tormented understanding of an impossible situation, and in my desperation I went and bought insanely expensive tickets for *The Lord of the Dance—Michael Flatley* in order to entertain Mother during her visit. But instead of seizing the opportunity to take a break from each other, Zola and Mother both insisted on going and ended up getting hammered in the local pub after the show. I never understood what happened, but assumed that Zola's wild nature had echoed the hysterical humor Mother would embrace after her third drink and abandon on the thirteenth.

Yet the cracks were starting to show. We'd moved abroad to get away from it all but somehow ended up with Icelandair's most common export; our apartment became a haven for binge drinking friends who wanted a weekend off, worn out and overworked, tormented by sleet and something they called "Despiceland Syndrome"—one of those viral concepts from some TV show that people used and abused to express their disdain for Iceland. I had no idea we had so many friends in Reykjavik and was taken aback by the constant turnaround on our living room couch of different bodies; naked, snoring, and even fucking. When an old classmate of Zola's from elementary school called and asked to stay while she held a three-week art exhibition on Grafton Street I was so miserable that I threw up on one of her paintings and took a thirteen-hour walk out of the city, ending up in a hotel room by an emerald lake complete with a couple of romantic swans. There was no phone in my room and I didn't reach Zola until the next afternoon. She forgave me, but that was the beginning of the end.

I still don't know why the move to Dublin was so ill-fated, what forces finally tore us apart. I had loved Zola with a fervor that I couldn't put into words, but that was the gauge for all my days and dreams for the future. When she left me I broke. I cried, filling up the glasses I downed in Dublin's hotel minibars until I returned to Iceland a ruined man, red-eyed and crushed by a despair I thought I could never shake. A couple of days later I moved in with Mother.

As soon as the plane takes off from Keflavik she turns to me, on her third drink, as if she'd been listening in on my thoughts: "You know, Trooper, nothing has grieved me more than love."

Chapter
3

Four hours later we found ourselves outside the terminal building in Amsterdam. Shards of sunlight pierced the thick cloud lining and formed a rainbow over the parking lot. I felt like I was in an ad for a cellphone company with a theme of Nordic happiness and that I should call all my friends at fantastic roaming rates. The filtered rays cast a gray hue over the morning and reminded me of Lóa, a school friend who'd abused tanning beds and ended up with melanoma. It turned out that I didn't have the maturity or strength of character to stand by her in her illness and she put an end to our friendship from her hospital bed, paler than she'd ever been, one foot in the grave. Years later, around the time Zola and I were breaking up, when I had as good as buried the incident, Mother pointed out that I was hardly likely to hold on to a woman when even the dying felt they were better off without me. She had a knack for putting the events of my life in context; the harsher the statement, the truer it rang. Like a veiled subconscious with make-up, she knew me better than the feet that carried me.

"I'll wait here while you find us a car," she said and sat down on a bench. I left her there with our luggage and walked toward an old fashioned car I'd spotted out in the parking lot. The car had a Libertas logo on its side doors and leaning against it was a short and slender man in his forties with black hair, dressed in a white shirt and khakis.

"Mister Hermann Willyson, sir?" he asked in English. "I am your driver. I shall drive you to Lowland."

"Hello," I said, offering my hand. "I think Mother and I need to check in at the hotel first and get rid of our luggage, if that's okay? My mother is, well . . . it's been a long journey."

"Very good, sir. I shall drive you."

I walked back to Mother, who was stubbing out a cigarette on the sidewalk. The driver followed and stopped by the bench. "Mam Briem, Mam, I am the driver," he said and smiled, picked up her bags, and walked back to the car.

"We have a chauffeur? How fancy."

I took her arm and led her to the car, which impressed her just as much as the driver. When we drove off he turned down the Bollywood music blaring from the radio. "Mam Briem, Mam," he said when we got out on the freeway.

"Eva," Mother insisted. "For heaven's sake call me Eva."

"Eva, Mam? OK. Does EvaMam want to go to the hotel, Mam, or straight to Lowland?"

"Whatever suits you best, dear. I'm up for anything."

She leaned back and stared out the window. The seats were soft and the view clear through the large, untainted windows that made Mother admire the vehicle even more. "We'll go to the hotel," I said, leaning toward the driver. "Mother needs to . . ."

"*Nei, nei, nei,*" she said slowly but loudly, with her legs stretched out over the backseat. "No special needs, *bitte schön*, not on my behalf. As if we're not perfectly fine here in this luxury?" She waved a cigarette over the driver's head to indicate that she would like to smoke in the car, and within seconds the interior became a version of my past. The acrid smell awoke memories of being carsick in Mother's friend's minivan during poorly-air-conditioned road trips. I rolled down my window and breathed in Holland. Mother was in her own world so when I pulled my head back into the car I felt duty-bound to strike up a conversation with the driver and asked about the car.

"It's an Ambassador, sir. Indian car. 1800 ISZ."

"Oh? I didn't know you could get them here."

"I brought it with me from Nainital, sir. That is my town in India."

"And did you drive all that way?"

"Exactly, sir. I drove."

"That must have been some road trip?"

"Yes, sir." He seemed determined not to be tricked into a lengthy conversation but after a long pause he added: "I got a new engine in Carta."

I liked this reserved driver. A man who drove over 6,000 miles across two continents and found the most notable part of the journey when he changed his engine, had to be a very responsible driver. The traffic thinned the farther we got from the city. The driver pointed to a sign in Dutch and turned off the highway onto a narrow road that cut through a rural area. Farmhouses appeared sporadically in the fields until we came to a place where a few buildings convened around a small church building. Next to the church stood a restaurant and a large house with the Dutch flag flying high. Two men sat on the porch in front of the restaurant staring into their beers while a young woman seemed to be giving them an earful, gesturing in frustration and then walking off. Spring was sneaking into Lowland. Squirrels nibbled on seeds by the roadside while the sun baked the winding track and disappeared behind the trees. In the outskirts of the hamlet lay an even narrower trail to a gate with the name "Libertas" on it, and an alley of trees running through the grounds. The driver got out to open the gate, then got back behind the wheel and burped like he had done every fifteen minutes since we left the airport. He would later explain that people who ate spicy food every day had a livelier gastric system than salad eaters and that there was no point in trying to contain the burping.

I felt my mind and body relax as we drove under the continuous canopy. It was serene, the weather was still, and nothing disrupted the silence except the soft purr of the engine. I rolled down the window again and felt the crisp coolness left by the morning rain seep into the car. The humid breath of the foliage made the earth smell of carbon, rotting wood, and the vegetation that winter had concealed beneath snow. I found myself staring at a few extremely thin men with golf clubs standing on the other side of the tree tunnel. They were ashen and almost transparent compared to the robes hanging loosely on their skeletal frames. Once in a while they stopped in the groves and swung their clubs without discernable results, like a bunch of happy corpses.

I'd warned Mother long before we set off that she might have to get over her fierce aversion to drugs; she would probably be handed a joint upon arrival. Mother still slept in an XXL T-shirt that said: "Just say NO!," a garment that our cousin Matti had given her after he learned that little Kiddi, his only son, had mortgaged the ancestral home to pay for his LSD habit. Ever since, Mother had detested recreational substances other than alcohol. She often talked about how awful and sad it was that she could not build a little summer cottage on the land she grew up on. The dealers had cheated her of that. They were thugs from Estonia and Lithuania who had invaded the country to ruin our youth, men who raped women and swindled the very land away from good Icelanders. Mother had never forgiven the Baltics for declaring independence during very difficult times in the history of the USSR. She blamed it on Iceland's former Minister of Foreign Affairs, Jón Baldvin Hannibalsson, "a lounge socialist who snuggled up to the conservatives as soon as he got the chance." And now these Baltic mobsters were flocking to Reykjavik with their dope, that's all the thanks we got for supporting them in betraying old Soviet Russia. Pimps and junkies, like the ones who corrupted little Kiddi. She would never be manipulated into taking these chemical death drugs that robbed good people of their health and reason. That road was a dead end: bankruptcy and emotional ruin.

"Old Lowland," the driver said and pointed to a handsome house at the end of the track. The grounds opened up as we drove on: yellowish fields sheltered by evergreens that spread out between whitewashed buildings. Rusty machinery grew into the ground, on top of which sat a lady enjoying an ice cream. The scene looked like something from Mother's subconscious on a good sherry day. She loved Fellini and Buñuel and some Czech fellow who made movies about pigs and old cars. It all reminded me of these friends of hers from the silver screen.

"Here, Mam," the driver said, looking toward the building in front of us. Mother's head seemed to pop out of the glass pane. She started and looked around.

"Jetlag, Mam," the driver said. "I don't know it myself but I've heard about it: some are unlucky and can't sleep, but you are very lucky, Mam. You slept on the freeway."

Mother, who was obviously still half-lost in her dreamy dialogue with the car window, looked quizzically at me: *Where are we?* The driver beat me to it: "It's very good for Mam to sleep, Mam. Now she is pretty for her meeting with Mister Doctor Frederik." She giggled at the word pretty and the Indian shot out of the car to open the door for her.

"Now, here we have a proper gentleman who knows how to treat a lady," she said, laughing as she got out. "May I ask how to address such a gentleman?"

"Ramji, Mam. I am Ramji the driver," he said and made his way to the steps that led up to the entrance of the building. Tall, French windows looked out into the yard and on the garret there were oval windows with opaque, industrial glass that reflected the surrounding landscape. A fountain with Renaissance style statues stood in the middle of the gravel-filled driveway where Ramji had parked the car. Mother gaped at the vision. While we waited to be taken inside, I told her that the house had been built in colonial times as a hunting lodge for a wealthy merchant, one of Rembrandt's clients. The master painter had probably spent some time in the house, making it one of the country's notable historical buildings.

"They'd like it here, Nikolaj and Julie," she said, referring to characters from a Danish drama series we watched back home on Spítala Street. "I do hope they make up. I think it's wrong of them to throw everything away because of one mistake. She just has to forgive him. So what if he strayed a little bit, don't we all? But this house . . . it's like Madame Antoinette herself should be strolling about somewhere. What a gem, Trooper. You truly are a genius."

Ramji came trotting back down the steps. "Is Mam rested?"

"Oh, yes. I think I'll actually have a little schnapps now." She fished out a miniature from her handbag, a bulbous little flask she called her "lifesaver," which she prized over other miniatures because it held 100 ml instead of the normal 50. She took a swig and then handed the flask to Ramji, who at first stared in disbelief, but then smiled and shook his head. Mother laughed and gulped down the rest of the contents. It had taken Ramji half an hour to establish a form of communication with Mother that I couldn't remember anyone else managing, even over several decades. My respect for this gracious, burping driver was constantly growing.

"We wait here until Doctor Frederik arrives, or Helga, Mam," he said.

"HelgaMam?"

"The director, sir, HelgaMam. She is a very clever lady."

As soon as he finished the sentence the door opened and out came a woman who surely had to be HelgaMam: she was short but sprightly, in a knee-length, green dress that emphasized her womanly curves, alert and without that affected elegance of career women that always lulled me into a drowsy state of composure. She strode down the steps and welcomed us warmly to Lowland.

"I am so pleased to meet you, Mrs. Briem, right? And Mr. Willyson? I'm Helga Wiestock. Our offices and the doctor's apartment are here on the second floor, but our reception room is downstairs. Would you like a refreshment?"

"I could do with a glass of white," Mother said in Icelandic and gave her hips a little shake. I had obviously made a mistake by not letting Ramji take us to the hotel. I was about to call it all off until the next morning when HelgaMam spoke.

"I have to apologize for the long ride. Ramji is an excellent driver but . . ."

"Oh, Ramji!" Mother exclaimed, fired up by her lifesaver. "What a wonderful man."

"I thought he'd take you to the hotel. If you'd rather come back in the morning then . . ."

"*Gar nicht*," Mother answered. "I never get jetlagged. I would appreciate a little schnapps or a glass of white wine."

"Of course!" HelgaMam didn't skip a beat. "My office is across the field. If you'd care to walk with me I'll tell you a bit about our work here. Then we'll drop in on Dr. Fred and see if he can't get us a drink."

"*Ein wunderbares Traum, glaubst du nicht, mein Schatz?*" Mother asked, refusing to acknowledge that I didn't understand her theater German. "I was just saying to my son that this is like coming to Versailles."

"I'm pleased to hear it, Mrs. Briem. Many of our guests prefer to stay at Lowland while others like being in the city. That's just the way it goes. You'll be staying in a hotel in Amsterdam, right?"

"To begin with," I said. "We're going to look for an apartment."

"You can see that not all mothers are as lucky as I am. He's doing this all for me, my Super Trooper."

The director grinned and we walked across the grass. She told us about the old cottages that were the servants' quarters before Libertas took over the estate and converted them into patient housing.

"We have six people staying with us now. Two from my country, then we've got Americans and Italians. We were twelve all in all until yesterday; counting myself, Ramji, the doctor, and the two German girls we have volunteering this summer, but our good, old Gombrowich departed last night."

"What?" Mother looked up absentmindedly. "Where did he go?"

"I think you're tired, Mother." I gave the director an apologetic look and turned back. "I think we should go to the hotel now and come back tomorrow."

"Not on my account. Is there really so much to do?"

"Not today really," HelgaMam said. "My office is over there and you're welcome anytime. If I'm not in you can call the number on my card, which I'll give you after you've met with the doctor."

"Ach, let's get this over with," Mother said. "You may think I'm a complete invalid like Emma Gulla, I mean she practically had to marry a doctor. But to tell the truth I can't really feel this so-called cancer in my leg. And definitely not after a little schnapps."

"Well, then we should go see the doctor."

She led us back to the mansion, up the stairs and into the doctor's quarters. The doctor sat behind a blue desk on the second floor and beamed at us when we entered. He was older and grayer than in the photo on the website, but easily recognizable nonetheless. He had an aura about him of times gone by that was hard to define. His clothes were strangely tailored, the waistband of his pants sat high on his gut, held in place with suspenders, and he wore an unbuttoned, powder blue doctor's coat.

"Welcome, welcome," he said, offering his hand. He suddenly stopped midair and stared intently at me. "What have we here?" he said and pointed to the mole on my temple. "Well, I'll be damned! Black Beauty. What a strange place for him. How wonderful!"

"Who's Black Beauty?" I asked, puzzled by the doctor's behavior.

"*Afrandarius erpexoplexis*, aka Black Beauty—because of the color—all the way from the vast Pacific. Yes, my friend, that mole you've got there is in fact a fungus, and not from Europe at all, no, it's quite remarkable. Very rare here and almost never seen on the face. May I ask how long you've had it?"

I told him that it appeared during my college graduation trip to Hawaii, where we'd gone hiking and I'd ended up with this lasting souvenir on my face. I'd stared at this thing in the mirror for the

31

past seventeen years and often tried to lance it, but never managed to remove it completely. I had to admit that it had never occurred to me to discover what it was.

"An old and loyal friend deserves a name, you can call it Black Beauty until you find another one. Truth be told, I would like to have a shot at it. I'm sure I could remove it with a bit of anesthesia and a jab. *Afrandarius erpexoplexis!* I have a considerable fungi collection. You won't have to worry about it—I won't kill it."

"My mole?"

"Sure. That's a real treasure," he said and tapped it lightly with his forefinger. "And it will take pride of place in my collection. Right next to *Ferflexus atarticus* and *Norgonakis felenferosis*. These are the great royal houses of fungi."

Mother cleared her throat.

"Ah, yes, well . . . Welcome to Lowland, it's always nice to have new people."

"I suppose that's the way it works?" she said. "Aren't people constantly kicking the bucket?"

"Oh, yes, death comes to us all. But it's life that matters, milady. Life. You should enjoy it, Mrs. Briem, and have help to ease your passing if all else fails."

"Anything but having my leg chopped off."

"That won't be necessary. But we are bound by the law. I cannot go beyond what my oath allows when it comes to foreigners. We sometimes send them to Switzerland, where they can offer assisted suicide to everyone. But we shall see. We should be merciful to the dying and offer remedies to those who still have hope."

"That's what Trooper tells me," Mother said, still a bit wary in the presence of the doctor. "And he also tells me that I shouldn't take offense if someone hands me a joint. But I can tell you straight away, doctor, that I do NOT do drugs."

"Well, cannabis seems to help most cancer patients, Mrs. Briem." The doctor chose his words with care. "And though it's fair to say that it does nobody good to smoke too much, I do find the reluctance in Europe to acknowledge the medical benefits of the Sativa remarkable. Ukrain on the other hand—well, I suggest that we start treatment as soon as possible, first thing Monday at the latest."

"Treatment? What do you mean?" We had discussed the Ukrain treatment numerous times back home, yet Mother still seemed clueless. "I didn't come to the Netherlands to become a patient."

"Of course not, you came to have fun, your son and I discussed this over the phone. But we cannot ignore that you do have a very serious disease to deal with. Ukrain does wonders in the fight against cancer. And as strange as the fear of the *Cannabis sativa* is, it is even stranger how much adversity my good friend Nowicky has had to contend with trying to market his remedy."

"Nowicky?"

"One of the great minds of our time. And my Swedish colleagues . . . I should think they had other things to worry about at the Academy. Ukrain on the other hand . . . Hmm."

"Trooper, tell the doctor I don't want any injections," Mother said in Icelandic.

"We've been through all this. You'll have more time, maybe a year."

"I refuse to be injected," she repeated in English.

"You are an intelligent woman, Mrs. Briem," the doctor said, "my glasses do not deceive me. The principle behind all our work here at Lowland is that life is more important than death. Nobody is forced to do something he or she does not want to do, but in your case . . . well it would be folly not to try the treatment. The cancer has not yet spread!"

"Trooper?"

"The doctor knows what he's talking about."

"Yes, but . . . injections. I just hate getting shots," she said in Icelandic and then switched to German: *"Ich dachte wir wollen einen Schnapps bekommen?"*

"That *is* the reason we came, Fred," the director said and smiled to the doctor. "The rest can wait until after the weekend."

"Yes, but not a day longer! I shall join you in the lounge for a toast and then we'll call it a day. Next week you can meet Helena and Steven. They'll invite you to Warmoesstraat and get you what you need. What do you think of the name of their shop: Pleasure Fountain? I think it is very smart, most fitting."

"Is that a brothel?" Mother asked making the doctor shake his head with laughter. He went on to explain that the Pleasure Fountain was Helena's herbal remedy shop.

"She'll fix you up with something to make you feel better," he said. "But now I want to make a toast to your arrival at Lowland and to better health. By all means try to enjoy your weekend. Only happy people stay at Hotel Europa. So have fun. *Grüss Gott!*"

Chapter
4

The first night in Hotel Europa I dreamt that Mother and I were Siamese twins. I moved to the left and she moved to the left. I tried to shake loose but my body sat still on her hips, which were also my hips. Instead of four legs, we each had one leg and between them was a phenomenon that bore a striking resemblance to Albert Grimaldi, Crown Prince of Monaco. We fell and sprayed forth a million tons of blood that flowed over the earth until it went dark. I dissolved into Mother's body—I was her and the entire galaxy at the same time. Gargantuan factories breathed black contagions over the world, and I knew they were her tumors; that was where the cancer lived. All I could do was run away. The factories turned into a white space without walls, where wine fountains in booths spewed bubbles at me. I could taste them and heard knocking . . . was I awake?

"Bankers!" Mother shouted, standing all dressed up by my bedside with a bottle of champagne in her hand. "Hah hah! I met bankers!" A wild lust for life glowed from her face and placed me squarely in the waking world.

"How did you get in?"

"In the end I had to have someone let me in," she answered. "*Mein Sohn*, I said, *Notfall*. It's incredible how you can sleep, Hermann. I've been knocking on your door since early this morning."

"You had someone let you in? What's wrong with you?"

"Trooper, I was trying to explain this to you. I went down for breakfast—like normal people do, and by that I mean people who don't sleep until noon—and what do you think I hear from inside the Gold Room? Icelandic, Trooper, Icelandic! There they were, five bankers drinking champagne. So I asked if I could join them. Well, it turned out they were having a meeting, but they gave me a bottle of this. Veuve Clicquot. Don't you like it?"

I could still taste the champagne and I realized that the final scene in my dream had not been a dream after all.

"Did you pour that into my mouth while I was asleep?"

"Something had to be done. You can't waste time sleeping in every day. Have you seen the weather outside? Just wonderful. And the view . . . You're a genius to have found us this hotel."

I got up and walked out onto the small balcony, which was just big enough for two chairs and a tiny table. It was a warm day. The sun seeped through the threadbare mist that spread over the city, immersing it in soft spring air. In my soul I was at homecoming, twenty years old, drooling alcohol at nine in the morning, convinced that within half an hour my body would be saturated with liquor and love for all the dimensions of the universe. We had decided earlier that the weekend would be an adventure, sickness banished from existence, and the only meaning of life would be to have fun until we dropped dead from happiness. Mother stared with fascination at the water. Even in her wildest soap opera fantasies, she had never imagined such luxury as we now enjoyed at

Hotel Europa: two-room suites with balconies and a view over the canal, bright lounges and sleeping quarters with mahogany beds, bathrooms with gold-plated faucets, and slippers.

"You mustn't envy me for getting the more elegant suite. The staff probably decided to put me in there, seeing as I'm older. I'll just light one up while you get dressed. As the bankers in the lobby said: Amsterdam, here we come!"

*

The first thing Mother mentioned when we walked out into the sunshine was the deep-rooted culture in the street landscape. From here, the brave adventurers sailed off for the Indies, and here the master painters had filled in the canvas of history.

"Not to mention all the crimes of passion and the orgies," she added. "Can you imagine all the sensations that have bubbled in these houses? Countless whoremongers and whores trying all sorts of sex. You almost want to jump through one of these windows and see if some ghost won't take you on. This is quite a change from Reykjavik with all those ceaseless Subway and McDonalds ads. Not to mention that horrible *Idol* thing. Why do people insist on being so devoid of culture in Iceland?"

We walked to where the hotel met the street and the Amstel River branched out, dividing into smaller canals. Three black kids stood rapping on the bridge, much to Mother's delight.

"Hold this, Hermann, I'm going to take a photo," she said, hung her handbag on me and skulked behind me with the camera. "I've often wondered how much more fun it would have been if I'd had you with a black man, Trooper."

"What?"

"Yes. It would have been such a nice contribution to the diversity of the population to have you a bit tinted."

"Ah. But would I have been me then?"

"As if you would have noticed? You wouldn't have given it any thought, just like you don't currently think about what it would have been like to be colored. That's the problem with having just the one life. I'll never really know what it's like to be Catherine Deneuve."

"The only thing you know is that you're Icelandic," I said and explained to her my theory that the nation's color chart, excluding the handful of immigrants in the restaurant business, could be divided into three categories. I belonged to the Porridge People—people who work indoors and therefore have the complexion of oat porridge in the first stages of souring. Then there were the Pig People—people who simply were the color of pigs, and finally the Prosperous People—orange people who had chemical skin treatments and worked in finance or media. The whole flock was descended from the same pale ape that discovered Iceland.

"Then you'll understand, my dear Trooper, what soul food it is for people like me who got their education in Fraülein Europa to finally have some diversity." She pointed to a tall, attractive older man on a bicycle. "You just don't see silver foxes like that in Reykjavik, not unless they're married or throwing up in some bar."

I promised to call the *Guinness Book of Records* to let them know. Almost everything we came across defied haters of beauty. The program was in full swing. It was highly unlikely that any mother and son in the history of mankind had ever had as much fun before noon.

To celebrate, she fished out her lifesaver and offered me a capful, which I gulped down as fast as I could. It tasted like every type of alcohol known to man with a touch of brandy in the foreground, which was probably what she poured into the flask the last time she filled it.

"Here, have some more," she said and got out a miniature she'd pocketed from the hotel minibar. "You could do with a pick-me-up."

"No more for now, thanks. I'd prefer a beer and some coffee first. How about finding a seat and having a look at the map?"

"Great idea, Trooper. If there's anything I've learned on my travels it's that you can never sit down enough . . . but I can't say I've ever had much use for maps. My map is in my heart."

I resisted mentioning her disastrous trip with the *Friends of Romania* group that ended with me flying to Slovakia to take her home.

"Here," she walked into a weird café where two men took turns frying pancakes and cutting people's hair. We got a table by a window looking out over the canal and ordered coffee and pancakes. "They've even got Internet here. Would you check my email for me and see if I've got any new messages?"

I agreed and asked for her password.

"Milan Kundera, one word."

"The poet?"

"He's a writer, Hermann. And not just the best writer in the world but also the most beautiful man I've ever set eyes on."

"Wow."

"I know. And so it's a great password. Not a chance I'll ever forget it."

I went through her mailbox, conscientiously reading aloud to her every single email, including a distraught message from Obed

Kanutsi, a wealthy Nigerian fellow who had been terribly wronged by an unjust government and modestly asked for 1,000 dollars to pay for his escape, promising, of course, to back the loan with very generous interests.

"We have to help him, don't we Hermann?"

"Nope. It's spam."

"But what about this watchmaker in Switzerland? Won't he be disappointed if I don't buy something?"

"These aren't personal letters, Eva. You don't have to feel bad about deleting them."

"If you say so."

After a short argument I decided to be the villain and deleted all her mail, checked my own inbox quickly and then played a couple of racing games for fun. An ad from *Russian Bride* flashed in the top right corner and immediately caught Mother's attention.

"Look at that, Trooper! You're being offered sex."

"Everything's available online now."

"What luxury for these young generations, to be able to just pick a prince from a website. Isn't there something for dying women in their sixties?" Mother laughed at her own joke but quickly turned serious again. "I mean it. Can't you find me a good man? Just for three months or so, can't be more than that if we're to have time for all those museums. The Cannabis Museum, The Museum of Torture . . . And Van Gogh! How are we going to manage all that?"

"You'll do that with the guy, I guess."

"You never know what these men are thinking. Like Jonas? Do you think he would have been interested in going to the Museum of Torture, limping about like some . . ."

". . . bondage gimp?"

"No, thank you very much! There was never any of that with Jonas. He was a terrible pervert of course, like most men, but nothing that was any fun. He just wanted me to stroke him, like you would a child's head. Which reminds me." She pulled a pack of condoms from her handbag: *Durex. Ribbed for her pleasure.*

"This, my dear, is for you."

"I'm not 15, you know."

"I have no idea what your age is when it comes to sex, Hermann, but I do know, because I'm a woman of insight, that there are temptations all around this city and it's always better to put safety first. Especially men like you who haven't seen much action lately."

"Oh yeah?"

"Yes. A man who mopes in his mother's attic and hardly ever leaves the house—unless you've been molesting the furniture it seems pretty clear that the only pleasure you've had in that area is that which you give yourself."

I took the condoms and put them in my pocket, claiming they wouldn't last me the week. The fact of the matter was that this analysis of my love life was sadly right on the money. Aside from the three weeks of whoring in Dublin after the breakdown, my sexual organs had indeed seen very little action. In my teens and well into my twenties I was so terrified by sex that I didn't dare seize the few offers I got. Globalization was a term I associated mainly with hep C, herpes, and AIDS. If I threw caution to the wind and slept with a woman it was only after double bagging my gear, which not only made it look bigger, but also like it had been given a shot of Tetraquinine. As a result, my sex life was mostly limited to masturbation—until I met Zola. When our relationship ended my mind was so infused with fantasies about the female body that the risk of Hepatitis didn't even deter me. A seriously drunk hotel manageress, a housewife with a furry animal, and a woman who at first seemed fairly run-of-the-mill but turned out to have an abundance of chest hair—I tried it all. The hibernation that my genitals had been in the last couple years of our relationship caused me to jump back into the saddle, a starved man with his raised meat sword, ready to poke any old potato. The little luck I'd been graced with in the looks department had run out and I had to rely on a different sort of charm. That meant that I attracted all sorts of freaks, women who were so alternative looking or with such unusual tastes and needs that sex became more of a behavioral experiment than an erotic act, which was probably the reason I gave it up after I moved back into the attic.

"But maybe I should go and see what's on offer in the Red Light District. I've heard that these gigolos can deliver orgasms on cue."

We emptied our cups and went back out to enjoy the lovely weather. I told her what came to mind as we soaked in the surroundings. Like that the house on our right was built by Jacob van Campen, the master of Dutch baroque. That the Royal palace from 1646, which Van Campen designed with Rome in mind, was an exquisite example of the golden age of architecture and paved the way for Wren's classicism.

"When your mind goes off, Trooper, it's like a tornado in Tangiers. One doesn't expect anything and then out of nowhere you whip up something like this."

"I just read that in a brochure."

"Yes, but how you remember all this stuff is remarkable. Someone whose only interest seems to be racecar games shouldn't know these things. I have no idea where you got this from—well, maybe your father. He's the only man I've known who got infected by STDs before ever having actual sex."

I didn't dare ask her if she felt that baroque was my Herpes, but she was right: absorbing and storing facts had always been my strong suit. They just seemed to stick like glue to my cortex and would not budge come what may: strong spirits, arsenic, and eating from Teflon pots and pans had absolutely no effect on my brain. I therefore possessed strange and bizarre knowledge about things I had no interest in or use of. I sucked up my surroundings without wanting to, like a vacuum cleaner with asthma. Each hemisphere of my brain was a capsule of non-cohesive and trivial information, a supermarket of information where wide-eyed people strolled the aisles in bewilderment, at a complete loss over what to do with all the merchandise. Knowledge was wasted on me. I was like a rich brat who receives a 1,000 TB computer for Christmas in order to play computer games while the physicist next door has to make do with an unreliable old laptop.

"I'm actually a conservative," I said, and was about to explain when a stinging sensation stopped me and I was blinded by tears.

"I'm so sorry, Hermann," Mother said, wiping away my tears. "That was a bit harsh, I'll admit that. I hit you."

"Wwwww?"

"Yes, but it was pure instinct. Since when are you a conservative?"

"No, I just meant that I get this huge computer when . . . Was that why you slapped me? It hurts like fuck."

"I'm sorry, Trooper, I couldn't help myself. But you're saying you're not really a conservative?"

I didn't answer but charged into the next bar to ask for some ice for my cheek. Mother followed me and offered to buy a very special drink with the money I'd given her earlier.

"It's fine," I said. "But I'd rather you didn't resort to violence whenever I say something you don't approve of."

"I know, Trooper. I apologize. It won't happen again."

We sat quietly by the bar and waited while the bartender checked his selection of specials. On Mother's top ten list of world wonders, a "special" drink came in third, after Milan Kundera and the Left Green Party. She defined the level of wonder by the alcohol percentage more than anything else, and the intoxicating effect the special had on the consumer. High acidity was a bonus but the main thing was to have the drink saturated with ethanol. The most common moniker known to the outside world is "cocktail," but she felt that it didn't do the drink justice because cocktails often seriously lacked the right amount of alcohol and were just a way to sell people overpriced sugar water.

"That's why it's necessary to be in direct contact with the bartender while he's mixing. It's nice to feel a bit tipsy sometimes even though you don't need to become drunk each time you have drink."

Because of Mother's familiarity with alcoholic beverages and their consumption she found it ridiculous when I showed signs of intoxication. She had even less of an understanding of being "hung over" or downright sick, as I tended to get from drinking. Anything more than a six-pack of beer could send me into an aimless walkabout in the tundras of self-loathing and regret. Mother was different. In her mind a half pint of sherry and some *Spätzle und Sauerkraut* were the best remedy for the sad syndrome others liked to refer to as a hangover. To her, eggs were served scrambled with olive oil and cognac. Mackerel was food you ate with a shot of rum. Plaice was a side dish with an egg yolk and pickled onion, but only if there was port in the yolk.

"Well, here we have some schnapps," she said, throwing back a shot of Bols, which was on the house as the bartender had failed to come up with a special. "This is just bad enough to prevent you from drinking too fast and yet it's good. God is in the tempo, as they say. I don't understand how you can go on drinking beer like this. Just like Willy—he'd never have a drink before noon and even then he'd always stick to beer. I suppose its like when I went to Sweden and they always had that Mellanöl. Disgusting drink. I can't say I've been hung over very often, but this was like drinking a hangover, it took forever to get a buzz."

Mother didn't really get drunk that often despite her considerably diligent intake of strong spirits. She often became what she referred to as "being pompette," slightly lightheaded. If the pompetting advanced to another level it was simply due to weariness from travel, and she did not enjoy going from one place to another so she drank to withstand it. But becoming inebriated, as a rule . . . that was over and done with. That sort of behavior flirted with forgetfulness and evoked a sense of loss and longing, for Germany, for instance. She'd learned this at AA meetings. She'd also learned that it was better to drink moderately every day than to sporadically gulp down gallons of liquor and lose all control. So each time I had a drink with her she smirked. I was obviously as inept at holding my liquor as Willy Nellyson. It was remarkable with the two of us, and yet neither of us were any good at sports. Both just as devoid of physical grace. She claimed that there had to be something seriously wrong with our composition, for she believed that golfing and tennis were at the core of the world of those who managed to live with a constant lack of alcohol. She was sure that all teetotalers were half-mad with energy and drive. These same individuals tended, however, to be rather boring, but they had that authority, like Ólafur Ragnar. He would never have become president if he'd been drunk all day.

"You're projecting," I said, finishing my beer. "You eat an entire apple in under a minute."

"That's only if I need vitamins."

"Nope, it's in your character."

"Oh?"

"You eat an apple in a minute and fast-forward through Nikolaj and Julie because you're so eager to get to the next bit. You're exactly the type who ends up in office."

"I suppose I'd be a very good president," she said dreamily. "And I'd bring about some change, I can tell you. For instance: I'd ban these self-jets that drive me up the wall back home. What is wrong with those people? People who never take the bus, but whiz by in taxcabs, waking you up in the middle of the night with all that noise, flying off to go shopping in Italy. I hate these people, just hate them." She slammed her fist on the table, quaking with anger. "Have you heard anything as idiotic? Flying to Italy to go to a shop? In a self-jet?"

"How do you think your precious banker friends got here? With a commercial airline?"

"Of course, they were generous gentlemen—I'm not talking about them. The people I'm referring to, Hermann, are all these self-jetting people smiling at you from the cover of gossip magazines. Who the hell do they think they are? Oprah Winfred?"

"Winfrey."

"What?"

I explained to her that the woman's name was Oprah Winfrey, but she had little interest in discussing her peculiar contribution to the language—self-jet, taxcab, Winfred; her creativity in this field seemed heightened when it came to foreigners.

"Do you see what I see?" She finally said and stood up, moving towards the window and pointing like mad. "Isn't that, what's her name . . . Helgamom? And Ramji! Yes, it's my Ramji! Ramjiminn!"

She ran out into the street and was out of sight before I knew it. I had no choice but to pay for our drinks and follow her.

Chapter
5

The Ambassador was parked farther up the street. HelgaMam and
Ramji stood next to a beautiful girl who introduced herself as
Helena, proprietor of The Pleasure Fountain, the shop the doctor had mentioned to us. We said hello, and a man in his thirties
stepped out of the car to greet us. He was the spitting image of the
doctor; for a second I actually though it was him after a night of
Botox treatments. Steven Turtleman was, in fact, a unique testimony
to the resolve of the sperm cell and its devotion to the genetic com-
pound of mankind. He had come to the Netherlands a couple years
ago looking for his biological father, Dr. Frederik, whom he had
found with the help of newly public documents on sperm donors
in the USA. Now he managed the Cannabis Museum in Amsterdam
and was the center's supplier of quality weed. His life story churned
out through his vocal cords like an unstoppable printing press until
Mother tapped his shoulder and interrupted him.

"It was so wonderful to see Ramji here that I just had to run,"
she said, breathless after the short sprint. "Isn't this a wonderful
coincidence, Miss . . . ?"

"Helena," the girl answered with a smile and said that Amsterdam was quite small; chance meetings like this weren't really that
unusual.

"I actually met some Icelanders this morning," Mother said. "Wonderful, generous men. But if you don't mind me asking, Mrs. Helgamom—is that your friend in the car?"

I'd noticed her wandering around the car randomly and realized that she'd been spying on the mystery man sleeping in the backseat.

"Duncan, our friend, yes. Have you met him?"

"No, I was just curious, he looks like a man I know. Well, I think it's best that Trooper and I let you go for now. We're going for a drink. Can you recommend a place?"

It turned out that the little party had just come from lunch at Shakespeare Fried Chicken, a branch of the restaurant at Lowland. They gave us directions to the place and we said good-bye.

"Did you see that man?" Mother asked when the car had disappeared around the corner. "The resemblance was striking."

"To whom?"

"Well, Milan Kundera, of course! *Nicht mehr und nicht weniger.* I don't think I've ever seen anyone who looks as similar to him as this Doonka does."

"Duncan."

"We'll see. But first we should get something to eat."

We stopped in front of a hand-painted sign and went into the restaurant. Shakespeare Fried Chicken was decorated in Medieval style: spears, shields, and coats of armor hung on the walls, next to which stood dark, hardwood tables with glossy, built-in benches. Aside from a few tourists, the clientele mainly consisted of two groups of men drinking beer, eating, and generally being loud.

"Since we didn't get our specials, Trooper, I think it's time we had a double schnapps and a single on the side," Mother said and laughed like she always did when talking about this passionate

49

quantity in the vast wonderworld of drinks: a double schnapps and a single on the side. I walked over to the buffet table and started shoveling food onto plates: shavings from a whole roasted pig stuffed with partridges, pheasants, and fresh herbs, a monster of a thing slathered in thick grease on a rack under flickering flames, surrounded by strips of bacon, vegetables, and potatoes.

"You're not going to leave that, are you?" Mother asked, pointing to my plate when were done eating. She had an irrational neuroses about leaving food. "We need a doggy bag."

"Are you planning to take this to rot up in your hotel room like you did in Slovakia?"

"Not at all, I'm going to eat it. That's going to last me three days, even more. You might laugh now but you won't be laughing tonight when I'll be trying to drag you back to the hotel, dead drunk and begging for food."

She said that her generation was used to having to think about more than just computer games and drugs, but despite her frugality in restaurants Mother did not have the qualms older people tend to have toward new things. Among the things she bought on her travels were chili seeds, Veneto mushrooms, and Mirin. In her opinion, the smartest use of an airline ticket was to buy something light that gained more weight the farther north you went. I told her to kidnap an Icelandic flight attendant and sell her in Yemen, but she ignored me.

"It makes no sense leaving it. Now go and ask the girl for a box, be a good boy."

I did as I was told. We paid the bill and left.

"There they are, there they are!" she shouted and ran to a ticket booth on the corner. "It's amazing that Icelanders are in charge of this. And I know them!"

50

In the booth window was a poster advertising the opening of IceSave in the Netherlands, an Icelandic bank that promised their customers higher interest rates than any other financial company in the country.

"Do you see what I see, Hermann? A bank launch. We're going."

"You hate self-jetters and bitch slapped me for being right-wing—and now you want to go for free food and drinks with some bankers."

"These are no ordinary bankers. They gave me champagne."

"Which they bought with all the money they made from the interest you're paying. Then you have to go abroad to get proper medical service while they sit here drinking."

"Don't be silly, Hermann. Why do you think these men have something to do with that? If you ask me, they probably came here to be free of the extortionary prices of everything back home."

"Eva, I'm telling you. These are the exact guys who are spending everything that people like you own on champagne and caviar."

"I don't understand why you have to be such a drag, Hermann. You have to learn to live a little. This here, for instance," she pointed to another poster that read: *Grave Night Fun. Karaoke. Wild Sex. Gay Men.* "Couldn't this be something for you?" The photo showed a group of leather-clad men at some sort of a karaoke rave. Mother thought this could be fun for me. I could sing songs with my friend . . . what was his name again? Freddy Mercy? "I'm joking," she finally said and hit me hard on the shoulder, as if the violent gesture would soften me up. "It's incredible how serious you can be. Have you seen all these wonderful posters?" She pointed to another ad on the booth with a picture of gray haired people sitting around a table, laughing with drinks in their hands. This poster read: *Single Caucasian Midlife Fun. Join us Saturday.*

"Isn't this exactly what we've been looking for?" she asked. "Like that Russian bride, but for people my age."

"You really want to go to a racist thing to find love?"

"I think you're misunderstanding, Trooper," she replied. "It only means that there'll be a limited selection. People your age are maybe used to having a million different types to choose from, but my generation can settle. I want to have a look."

I tried to talk her out of it to no avail, and watched her hand over 20 euros for two tickets. "Just landed and already whisked away to a ball."

"You seriously don't find this a tad offensive?"

"What do you mean," she said, preparing herself for yet another of my lectures on political correctness. "What is it that you find so racist about it?"

"It's a ball for single, middle-aged white people. Don't you find that a bit, I don't know—Hitler and his friends throwing a party?"

"No, Trooper, I think you're reading too much into this. This simply means that it's a get-together for people who like to meet other people with a similar background. It could just as well be for black people. Then it would also read: For single, middle-aged *black* people. I'm sure they have those too."

"I'm telling you—you've just bought tickets to some sort of neo-Nazi gathering."

"You can be so melodramatic," she laughed. "Or do you really think that of your mother—that I'm a neo-Nazi? I, who played Herta Oberhauser in a very controversial play?"

I turned away from her and let my eyes drown in the foreignness of the street. One of the many things Mother couldn't stand was the rigidity younger people had toward the multiplicity age. It was as if young people didn't understand that each generation had its own discourse and ways. She didn't attack people who talked about Down Syndrome, even though she herself had grown up in a world where people like that were simply called "retarded." What young people didn't understand was that people were different, the generations so unlike in their actions and attitudes. She knew this even though I didn't grasp it—which was understandable as I was raised by the Internet and TV, disgusting brainwashers that prevented everyone from having an independent opinion.

"You're changing the subject," I said. "When some guy is standing out in the street inviting everyone, except black people, to come to his party—that's racism."

"Hermann, do I have to spell it out for you? Just because some people have more things in common than others does not mean that the same group hates everyone else. Like your cousin Matti, who loves America more than anything. He's completely different from me, yet I don't hate him."

"It's just obvious that it's not right. I won't go near this."

"Fine. I'll go alone. I'll take Ramji with me."

I muttered that Ramji would be beaten and put in a cage before she even got to the bar, but Mother said I was being a spoilsport and became agitated.

"I don't understand what's gotten into you, Hermann. I suppose it's something repressed to do with Zola. I would like to point out, in answer to these insinuations, that I made you participate in that charity race for Africa, remember? Maybe that was racist of me, Hermann? Was it?"

She concluded by telling me that this was in fact just a difference between generations, that people her age tended to be more patient because they had seen so much, like the canned fruit that she ate for desert at Great Aunt Edda's house—it wasn't very exciting, but you made do, because that was simply what you were given. I knew that moments like this defined my role on this trip—I was to calmly nod and smile at everything Mother said even though it made my stomach churn. I just couldn't. So after stating that eating canned fruit was, in my opinion, not comparable to seeking out black people and setting them on fire like her middle-aged Ku Klux Klan buddies did, I jumped onto a bus and let the dusty daylight settle into an uneasy silence. Mother followed, but didn't look at me. I felt woozy.

"Probably best to forget it," I said. "Write off all aggression and get a bit drunk. I know that you're not a racist, just like you know that I'm not a right-wing conservative. Let's get off at the next stop, find a bar, and see who can order the most interesting round."

"You can be such fun, Trooper. When you want to be."

I pressed the button and whisked her out of her seat. We walked out into the dwindling daylight and found Papeneiland, one of the city's oldest pubs, a perfect place to get tanked and quench Mother's thirst for historic places at the same time.

"If you're going to order a special, make sure to get a double," she called to me as I stood with my eyes fixed on the bar selection, determined to bring her a drink so inventive that it would blow her mind. This would be a world of wonders in a glass, the perfect blend of liquids, nostalgia's answer to the gratification of alcohol. I asked for a Donkey, a Cow, and a Frozen Fox, three cocktails that all bore witness to the influence of the agricultural industry in Iceland at the time when the intentional diluting of strong spirits started. The bartender was irritated by my special requests, but finally conceded to serving up a regular Bloody Mary, pouring an incredible amount of vodka and tomato juice into a cocktail shaker with some pepper and Tabasco. He got two pint glasses, filled them up, and threw in some ice and celery sticks. Quite pleased with the result, I walked back to our table and raised the glasses when Mother looked up.

"Ahh, Maiden's Blood? I don't think I've had Maiden's Blood since Matti had that tomato farm. Mmm, this is really good, much better than Matti's. Strong."

"I asked him to be generous with the vodka."

"Good for you, Trooper. Like old Edda used to say: When you make a special order, it better be special. No need to be shy about asking for that little extra shot."

We toasted each other in the glow of candlelight while the place gradually filled with people in intimate conversation with the night. Fueled by the vodka I became sentimental, let my mind wander through the past, not unlike the TV shrink Dr. Phil, according to Mother. I needed to help her find a man.

"I suppose the only solution is to find a gigolo. The men here in Holland seem as uninteresting as the ones in Reykjavik. Like that doctor. Seems completely asexual."

"You can't expect the doctor to hit on you during your examination."

"Is there something wrong with hoping that the few men who stray into my life make the tiniest of efforts?"

I had to admit that this lack of sexual harassment truly was a travesty, but she threw her hands up in frustration and asked me to give her a break.

"'Sexual harassment.' Ach. Another term invented by your sanctimonious generation. No wonder we're having a hard time picking up men, except for cold fish like Emma Gulla. She just orders them from catalogs."

"Isn't she the one that's always so happy?"

"Oh, Trooper, what do I know? I've just never been able to figure out love. Maybe it's just for boring people. Do you think that's it? That love is just for boring and ugly people like Emma? Look at the two of us."

We stared into the flickering night and called out to the melancholy, to the nostalgia that lived in the newly fallen darkness and the lights, in the crowds and the stars, in all these endless possibilities that didn't find their way to us, but planted us here, mother and son, each with a pint of special.

"When you think about it, Trooper, at the end of the day—we've at least always had fun. Now tell the bartender to turn off this noise and play some real dancing music. Soon I'll be dead and have less time for dancing, but tonight we dance. On the tables and up into the ceiling, like this, until the lights go out. We'll dance, my dearest Trooper. Just dance!"

Chapter

6

On Monday morning the focus returned again to matters of life and death, Ukrain or no Ukrain.

"Whether to take up arms against the fall of Spring? And the world of Summer—or to suffer the frost?" Mother recited poetry between bites of bacon, along with quotations from *The Iron Lady*, the controversial play about Nazi nurse Herta Oberhauser; anything to divert her attention from the upcoming doctor's visit. In her opinion she was going to suffer nothing less than a sadistic blitzkrieg by a professional torturer. Whenever I tried to discuss her treatment she would turn on me and ask me to leave her be; she needed peace and quiet to recall Herta's defense monologue. She would then go into detail about her erratic sleeping patterns, noises in the hallway that had woken her and how she had retreated onto the balcony with a glass of red wine around three in the morning. That had led her to open her book—*Catherine the Great, a Biography*—which turned out to contain some quite racy revelations of the Empress's extensive debauchery.

"She had her fun with poor Grigori for a few years, a perverse little youngster with a cock like a horse. When she got bored with him she made him bring her new lovers. By the truckload—imagine the luxury. There was something inherently wrong with her. The woman was insatiable."

I didn't have much to say on the matter, but pointed out that we really needed to get up to our rooms; the doctor would arrive any minute.

"Why do we have to do this? I find it terribly unfair to have to get all these shots on top of everything."

"Don't worry about it. The doctor is so used to giving injections that you won't feel a thing."

"Oh I'll feel them! It's serious business having someone stab you with a needle."

Since she seemed determined to view the doctor's visit as pain and suffering, I decided to let him cut off Black Beauty to ease the strain. My plan was to laugh off the jab to show Mother how easy it was. In the end I had to suppress my panic because the doctor was afraid he'd jab me in the eye if I didn't sit still.

"There!" The doctor said when he finally managed to stick the needle in the right spot. "Now we let the anesthetic take and meanwhile turn to the big matter."

He walked across the room in his green tailcoat, a flat tweed cap on his head and knee-high leather boots on his feet, and fetched a small case he'd left at the door. The locks on the case clicked open and he took out a tray with numerous small medical bottles that were marked: UKRAIN 5mg – 1 AMPOULE AM TAG. He produced needles, cotton wool, and gauze from a small leather pouch. He placed everything onto Mother's bed, took off his coat, and sat beside her. He then tied a rubber tube around her upper arm and used his fingers to find a suitable vein.

"Now, Mrs. Briem, I know that you don't like injections but I can assure you that my needles are the least painful injections available for Ukrain shots. You saw how easy it was for your son."

"Trooper is completely ignorant when it comes to injections. Is there really no other way? Can't I just drink it?"

"No, I'm sorry, the drug really has to be given intravenously if it is to work. You will need a daily shot for five weeks to begin with. After that we'll have to see, depending on how your body reacts to the treatment. There, we're done!"

Mother stared in astonishment at the doctor, like a person who'd just woken to find they'd slept through a war. "What? You're done?"

"Yes, all done."

"Did you see that, Trooper? How he did that? I must admit I didn't feel it a thing. You're obviously no Nazi, doctor."

"Pleased to hear that."

"You see, I played Herta Oberhauser once, she was a nurse who used needles to torture people. She was as obsessed with needles as Catherine the Great was with lovers. It truly is a miracle, doctor, that you're already done. I could visit the Museum of Torture now. Show them how to take it."

She stood up and poured herself a schnapps, her face like an atom bomb indicating the travesties awaiting the city's museums. The left side of my own face was steadily becoming more paralyzed. I felt like I'd fallen asleep after drinking glue.

"Look at you!" she said and pointed at me. "Quivering like a leaf over a petty mole! I've been telling my son for years now that not all women are into men with moles."

I made vague grunting noises in protest and used strong gestures to strengthen my case.

"It's true, Trooper. That mole has overshadowed everything that is charming about you."

"Oh?" I managed to snort despite the numbness. "Then I must declare that many women are into fungus."

"I must invite them into my museum one day," the doctor said and slid the knife up to my right temple. "This little guy will have pride of place in my collection. Even such a tiny organism can grow up to two or three inches if cultivated properly."

I didn't know what kind of psychedelic drug the good doctor had mixed into the local anesthetic, but I suddenly went cold at the sight of the knife, no longer so sure that Mother's claims of the inherent sadism of the medical profession were unfounded. Wasn't there something perverse about a man who collected abnormalities from people's faces?

"I'm not sure we should do this," I stuttered, shying away from the knife. "Maybe we should let Black Beauty stay in his natural environment?"

"You won't feel a thing and the cut will heal in a couple of days or so," Dr. Frederik said, ignoring my protests. "There we go! Here he is."

The mole fell from the blade onto the petri dish, where it disappeared under the lid.

"This calls for a toast," Mother said and poured us drinks. "To my health and to Trooper's love life, which should now take a turn for the better. I must say, you're a fine doctor, Doctor. I know a lot of old timers who're bound to fall ill any day now, and when they do I'll tell them to come to you. This has been such an experience."

When the doctor was gone I left it to Mother to prepare for the Museum of Torture. I had a date with Helena the homeopath, who had put together a potent mix of herbal remedies, by order of the good doctor, to maximize Mother's love of life. The store was in Warmoesstraat, in the very heart of the Red Light District, and was famous for being the first Smart-Shop in Amsterdam, selling a weird blend of sex toys and alternative medicine. I finally found the store after wandering through a maze of canals and tall, narrow buildings leaning curiously over the streets. The space was tight and cut in half by a long table around which the customers stood, examining the merchandise. I was growing quite curious about an electrical cervix when a blind German lady bumped into me and apologized in her native tongue. I can't say I was surprised that the first person I met in the sex shop was German. I had learned of Germany's extensive interest in sex from watching the TV series *Liebe Sünde*, available on Mother's tattered VHS tapes back home. An old friend of hers in Mainz sent her the tapes in return for flatbread. Over time the collection of *Liebe Sünde* grew rather impressive, and on occasion I had ended up watching the shows with her and finding out the latest developments in sex gadgets. Mother leaned toward the unabashed German way of discussing latex and insisted it would do me good to follow the series.

"*Guten tag.*" The shopkeeper had no doubt heard my exchange with the blind woman and figured that I was German, too. She pointed to an egg, a *Spitzen-Ei* that I had picked up from the floor, and encouraged me to speak my own language.

Overwhelmed by my lack of linguistic cunning, I backed out into the street and right into the arms of a madam. "I give you everything, good hands, good tongue, nice ass." Terrified of being rude I felt I should accept at least some minimal service, but to my relief she turned to the next passerby when I hesitated. I was bathed in the glowing red lights from the whorehouses all around me; it suddenly felt like Amsterdam was nothing but a pit of hookers, trannies, and packs of Italian men. A gigantic African man with a street organ offered me a piece of hashish in exchange for my jacket, and the hooker turned her attention back to me. The city was so overrun with price-tagged sex that I wanted to teleport to Ikea. People on their way to work squeezed past teenaged girls who choreographed the mundane reality with pornographic moves on their smoke break. Someone had procured them from Brno, Bangkok, or Budapest, dragged them out of their parents' tiled kitchens, smelling of porridge and sweat, shown them their Mercedes and fucked them all the way into the red booths. Like most people, my mind strayed regularly toward sex, but now in the middle of the orgy where everything was for sale, I just wanted to get out of there. Then I realized that I still held the *Spitzen-Ei* in my hand, so I stormed back into the shop, setting of the alarm that for some strange reason had not sounded when I had stumbled out with the thing. I forced a smile and waved the object in the air. *"Nur meine Ei."* Finally I managed to tell the shopkeeper that I was looking for Helena.

"Through there," she said, pointing to a beaded curtain. Behind it was a small space where the alternative medicine was kept. Helena sat on a high stool in heated discussion with a short man in a white suit. She was pointing to the curtain and seemed to be ordering him to leave. He turned away quite calmly, greeted me with a smile, and walked out.

"What was that?" I asked and handed her back the book she'd hurled during the argument.

"I can't talk about it," she said and snatched the book out of my hand. "He has a prescription from Fred, because he treats everyone the same, and then the little shit uses the opportunity to insult me with his preaching. I'm going to close up for a bit. Let's go for a coffee somewhere."

She grabbed a bag from under the counter and led me past a sales stand on the floor, where I managed to knock over a display of vitamin drops.

"How big is that space?" I asked when we were safe and sound out in the street.

"Forty-three square feet. I rent my little nook from the owners of the store. All modern commodities for 600 euros."

"For forty-three square feet?"

"That's Amsterdam for you. All space is infinitely expensive. There's a reason for perversions like fisting. Everyone is trying to save space by holing up in someone else's ass."

I found fisting a farfetched result of extortionate real estate prices, but Helena continued ranting and pointed to the next street corner where two small businesses—Asian Sexy Fetish and Dental Surgery 4U—shared a space. Above the business was a low window with a sign that read "Te huur": For Rent.

"The height of the ceiling in there is just over five feet and yet that dump can be rented out. In fact, it's the perfect place for toothless dwarf-whores."

"Doesn't it bother people that there's porn everywhere they look?"

"People can get used to anything and everything. I know a lot of people who find porn quite mundane and think of sex shows as a form of theater. The human race is just a species of ape in fancy clothes. We don't need Darwin to tell us that."

We went around the corner and then back into a vibrant shopping street where shopkeepers and fast food vendors nodded to us as we passed. Helena greeted everyone like a street kid and I got the feeling, as we talked more and walked farther, that she belonged both everywhere and nowhere. She had a room in Lowland, had a little space in a shed at Highland, slept on the couch in three differ-ent places in Amsterdam—depending on which friend could accom-modate her at each given time—and camped out at the shop when she had nowhere else to go. She claimed to be between decisions, under the influence of indistinct periods of time that she wasn't sure were beginning or ending.

"Pleasure Fountain is busier than many other Smart-Shops be-cause of the people Fred sends to me. I've managed to make a living from this even though I don't make enough to rent an apart-ment. Things tend to take time with me. I'm half done with medi-cal school, but I'm not sure I'll ever finish."

"But you're just in your early twenties, right?"

"Twenty-three."

"Halfway to becoming a doctor and you claim to take your time. Compared to you I'm a fetus."

"No. I'm gradually fucking things up for myself. Maybe I need several years to reach a conclusion."

"You're way too young to worry about this stuff."

"You're never too young to worry. Only the sublimely spoiled don't worry. When I was twelve I was put into foster care in High-land and on my thirteenth birthday I decided to take over from Fred when I grew up. I was going to run the center and change the world, do all the stuff he only dreamt about doing. But life is complicated. You start to worry."

While we roamed around the district looking for a good café, Helena told me about the operations in Lowland. I already knew that Fred founded Libertas in the sixties, but neither the brochure nor the website disclosed its rather romantic origins. As a young man, Frederik had left his hometown in the Swiss Alps where his family ran an established hospice for the terminally ill. The young doctor fell out with his father and took off, travelling around Europe studying new discoveries in cancer research. A few years later Frederik had made a bit of a name for himself with his research into cell division in fungi. His father, who was a proud man to a fault, paid out Frederik's inheritance to convey the message that they were incommunicado from then on. Fred's road led to Amsterdam, and from there, to Lowland, where all the buildings were falling into disrepair. He bought the estate and still had enough left from his inheritance for renovations and equipment. And that was how the Dutch Innovative Research Center started, focusing on cancer research and treatment. People came from all over Europe to undergo treatment with the new methods. Dr. Fred wanted to found a different hospice from the one his family ran in Switzerland, and the neighboring estate, Highland, played a big part.

"Duncan had a commune over there," Helena explained. "He came here with some hippy dream after a family dispute in Scotland. He and Fred became fast friends. Duncan wrote a novel based on it, the proceeds are still his main source of income. You saw him the other day, snoring away in the car."

"Ah, yes, him! So he *is* a sort of Milan Kundera after all."

"I don't know about that. Duncan hasn't written much more than that novel and numerous updates to the book for each reprint. It keeps him going because the book is pretty popular with the new age crowd. It sells as some sort of self-help guide. But that's how Libertas came to be. When patients got ill at the cancer center, Duncan would bring them weed and the commune sort of merged with the center, creating a hospice like no other. If people want drugs, they get drugs. Fred monitors the reactions, keeps a log, and administers the correct doses. The dying have nothing to lose in his opinion, but not everyone agrees with him on that."

She fished out a newspaper clipping from her bag with a photograph of the center, and a printout of an English translation with the heading "Death is Everyone's Business."

"I thought you'd maybe like to see this, just to know that people are not all of the same opinion when it comes to Lowland. This is an interview with the guy I was arguing with in the shop, Arthur van Österich. I translated it for you, listen."

She put on a pompous face and started reading to me the quote I would later paste into my diary about the trip:

> People who think that death is entertainment need to think again. If people insist on comparing life to a play they should realize that it can never be anything but a tragedy. The final act, the last setting, is the great crescendo of our suffering. To think that we can ease it by dulling the senses and numbing the pain is absurd. And I have to ask: Should an institution, the main goal of which is to do just that, have the power to deny people the last hope of conviction? Death is not a show. It is the most significant event of our lives.

"Is this aimed at Lowland?" I asked when she'd finished reading and handed me the clipping.

"Lowland, Fred, Helga. Van Österich waltzes in and out of the center as if he's the one and only authority on the act of dying, and then he attacks people from some philosophical point of view."

"Who is this guy?"

"Arthur van Österich is the Netherland's top academic in palliative treatment philosophy. He's been writing about this stuff for over 40 years, almost ever since Fred started running the hospice. Now he's dying himself, and he's determined to be remembered.

He's milking it for everything he's got—he attends events hosted by the Minister of Health and has his picture taken. He wants everyone to have a right to decide when they die, but because he's Arthur van Österich, self-appointed heir of Schopenhauer, he insists that this right must not be abused; you may not die *the wrong way*. I, however, think that he believes that everyone's death but his own is quite meaningless. He's said it himself: "First people don't know how to live and then they don't know how to die." The worst thing is that Fred just chooses to ignore this stuff. He's wholly occupied with his own research and the rest just doesn't matter to him."

"But doesn't the director respond?"

"She thinks Van Österich is entitled to his opinion like everyone else. The fact that he's dying gave him a chance to check into the hospice, and now he's using that as an excuse to tear us down. What's it to him if I give people some pills to make them feel a bit better?" She still seemed agitated after the run-in at the shop. "I'm not saying that he hasn't done any good, like his website—you won't find better information on euthanasia anywhere else. But I don't think that people should make up protocols for how other people should die. Fred lets people die the way they want to, and he's rewarded for his kindness with attacks from people like Van Österich. People who hate cannabis and think the Netherlands are far too liberal. Which reminds me . . ."

She placed the bag from the store in her lap and started arranging its contents on the table; little boxes and vials with peyote, O-3 bubbles, and calmus.

"And this will bring joy and happiness to all?"

"If bliss can be bottled, then yes. I have to run."

Chapter
7

The sun disappeared behind clouds as I walked down Warmoerstraat. The salt-and-pepper sky cast silhouettes on the pebbled pavement and sent my central nervous system on a journey to my shared past with Mother. Images of Great Aunt Edda and my cousin Matti floated by, saturating my brain with such sudden melancholy that I fled into the next ice-cream parlor and gorged on half a quart of mint sorbet.

I hadn't had much time the past few weeks to consider what the near future had in store. Each day brought new challenges that called for action rather than thought. I surrendered to existing without sensing the thin red line separating me from total ignorance, only just making out the obscure path laid out before me. Was I starting to resemble one of those pathetic people who needed to be followed by cameras while they ruined their lives, planted next to an older individual in some bus on the road to nowhere and tested to the verge of a nervous breakdown, all for some entertainment network? The idea melted into my mint sorbet and drowned in a high-pitched shout from nearby. On the other side of the street, Mother sat in a café with a tall, slender, middle-aged man. He was dressed in jeans and a bright green shirt.

"Trooper! Trooper!" She gestured to a chair and told me that they'd just been to the Museum of Torture and that they'd sat down in Warmoerstraat in the hope of bumping into me. She and Tim were going to enjoy some "hash-jazz" and insisted I come with them. "Have you two met? Tim, do you know Trooper—*mein Sohn?*"

He got up, smiled and introduced himself as Timothy Wallace, a patient at the hospice. "Tim was with Ramji when I called to ask him to drive me to the museum," Mother explained. "I told him to join me on the museum tour—it was on the way to the hash-jazz anyway. Of course it's up to you what you do, Trooper, but I wouldn't want you to miss out on this opportunity. As you well know, I don't smoke hashish myself, but when a single man escorts you to a museum and offers you some hash-jazz you really can't turn them down."

She added that she felt a certain empathy and closeness in the company of a dying person. She and Tim shared something that I unfortunately—or rather fortunately, perhaps—could not understand, and even though she had every intention of beating the illness, she felt there was something remarkable in meeting Timothy Wallace, a cancer patient from Missouri, and to share with him a certain fate. I smiled at the man and looked for coded signs in his face asking to be rescued from this situation, but he seemed to be enjoying it and told me he would try to keep Mother out of trouble.

We said our good-byes, and after walking a few times around the alleyways of Warmoerstraat I found the Cannabis Museum in a low building on the corner of Pijlsteeg. Before I got to the door, a large group of Mexicans piled in and I ended up at the back of a long, slow line in the dimly lit entrance. The lighting reminded me of Daniel, my former colleague, strangely gray and diluted, yet persistent. To heighten my torment, Céline Dion's face filled a screen in my line of sight with the accompanying sinking-ship-music blasting from the speakers overhead.

"Six-fifty," the girl at the ticket desk said, handing me a ticket.

"I'm here to see Steven Turtleman," I said. "Please let him know that I'm here."

She didn't react at all, just stared at me through a month's buildup of make-up and then finally pointed to the bandage on my temple and asked if I'd been in a fight. I explained to her that apparently my face was an appealing destination for fungi and repeated that I wanted to see Steven. I looked around the lobby while I waited, managed to get tangled up in a display of teas, and stumbled through a side door with a *no-entry* sign between my legs.

"Sir," the doctor's son came to my rescue, clamping a steadying hand on my shoulder. He helped me out of the closet and led me through a room with an herb garden and a relief of the Chinese Opium Wars. Our journey ended in an office with red walls, where he took off his jacket and offered me a seat.

"BodySnatch," he said and held up a small container, "is the only stuff that truly works for burning body fat. You know all these products: Fatodity, Feroxycut, all these countless thieving drugs on the market. Because that's what this shit does—steals your money and stashes it in some offshore account! But not BodySnatch." I had no idea where he was going with this so I just sat quietly and let him go on about the merits of the magic in the small container. "You were thinking of thirty boxes," he said, "I think you should take sixty."

"You think she really needs that?" I asked, realizing he might be confusing me with someone else. "I'm Hermann Willyson, Eva Briem's son. I'm here for the grass."

Steven's insistence gave way to surprise, his jaw hanging half way down his chest as he shuffled through some papers. "Willy-son!" he finally exclaimed, realizing with relief that I was not Mr. Bryn Robben from Trim Center, but the man he'd met last Friday by Ramji's car. "Wow!" he said, "To be honest I'm not so sure that BodySnatch really works, so it's good that you're not Mr. Bryn Robben."

I asked him what would happen when the real Mr. Robben came knocking and he said he was going to fatten himself up. Retailers of fat burning supplements would be fascinated by the ad campaign he had planned for BodySnatch.

"*Before and after BodySnatch.* I'm going to get some after shots done now, then I'll put on 20-25 pounds and do the before shots. Mr. Bryn Robben won't be able to resist. He'll go for sixty boxes."

He went on talking about his brilliant business plan and pointed to a La-Z-Boy with a double wire system attached to it. One of the systems was hooked to a cooler containing cream and a mobile funnel while the other one was tied to a tap to rinse the funnel after use. The whole set up reminded me of a story I'd read in Derek Humphrey's *The Final Exit*. It was about an electrician in Seattle who wanted to take his own life. He placed a light sensor in the windowsill of his hotel room, hooked it to explosives in his hat and then waited for the sun to rise. When it did, the wire got hot, detonating the explosives, which in turn blew off his head. Steven's cream machine was not as sinister a weapon, but the mechanisms were similar. When he sat back in the chair and popped up the footrest it pulled on a wire, moving the funnel to his mouth and the liquid poured straight down his throat, no swallowing needed. I pointed out that gorging on *Spätzle und Sauerkraut* in addition to regular sherry marathons for a few weeks would have pretty much the same effect, and might even be a healthier way to obesity, but he dismissed the suggestion with an aggressive wave of his hands.

"I hate food."

He stood up, retrieved an envelope with some grass, poured us tea, and began recounting his life story with the same enthusiasm as during our first meeting. In a relatively short time he'd lived in six foster homes, spent four months as an errand boy on a chicken farm, and a couple of months as a part of Dick Cheney's security team. His love for older women was laced with memories of a summer job in an underground bunker, where the only piece of furniture was a massage bench. He admitted that even though his native country was one of the greatest places on earth, it also contained some of the strangest people on the planet. It was good for business that Europeans were gradually catching up in weirdness, but there really was little comparison. For instance, he doubted that there were many Dutch men who would have their penises surgically removed and grafted onto their arms as a number of his compatriots had done.

"What? Why?" I asked, gaping more and more as our talk went on.

"Daddy Harold was an expert in penis enlargements. Had his own practice. The penis is grafted onto the arm so it won't die during the procedure."

"What if Harold died during the procedure? Would the patient have to leave with his penis on his arm?"

"Precisely, Mr. Willyson," Steven said and nodded his head knowingly.

Chapter
8

The next couple of weeks passed quite peacefully. Mother would kick-start the day with a dose of Ukrain, we'd have doughnuts and coffee at the hotel, take a walk, visit a museum, or catch a canal bus. I'd drop in on Helena at the Pleasure Fountain for a chat, and acquaint myself with Steven's stock of various supplements. Smoking sessions on the small balcony ensured smooth sailing into the realm of dreams after an evening out at one of the local bars. Then a new morning would break and the worldview was as round as the planet turning on its axis.

I decided to swallow my pride and reward Mother for her gallant and stoic resignation to the Ukrain treatment and take her to the Nazi ball. My drinking session started early in the afternoon with a private one-man Vodka Tournament in the hotel bar. Dmitri, my friend behind the counter, mixed up an orgy of fruit in his shaker and poured me shots like both our lives depended on it, and agreed that if there ever was a need to get shitfaced to survive an evening, this would be the occasion. A young Asian girl sat at the other end of the bar, petite and lithe, with suntanned legs that seemed to go on forever from underneath her red dress. I had been staring at them for a while when she came and sat next to me.

"You like Shaloo? Shaloo not free. Shaloo *expensive*. Shaloo make *change*."

I stared at her. I had supposed that such a feminine transsexual would choose to go stealth, but Shaloo had no qualms about having once been a man. She took a different stance.

"Shaloo always be woman. Dick no difference, she reverse it."

"I apologize for being so old fashioned," I said, "but to me my dick is all I have to prove that I'm a man."

"Darling, it in the heart! You decide what you are. I Shaloo, Night Queen. You tell me who you are."

"Trooper," I said. "My cardiologist tells me that I have the fat percentage of a sixty-year-old woman."

"You joker, Trooper. I hear it. You buy Shaloo drink?"

"Sure, but just the normal price. I recommend My Bloody Fucking Valentine. Or Brain Damage."

She settled on Brain Damage and we made a toast. After a short and rather interesting discussion about Thai sex change operations I ventured to ask how such a bright and beautiful person ended up in prostitution.

"Girl like me? Darling, I no get much money in other place. I fancy lady, I need *expensive* dress. I have high standard. Only men fifty years or older. Only five star hotel. No bondage!"

"No bondage?"

"Too risky. But for you, darling . . . anything!"

She laughed and said "fuckyfucky," which made me laugh, too, ready to drown in the infinite, shimmering beauty of this face. I felt that I might have to reevaluate my place on the gay-scale Mother used to distinguish the different levels of gayness of male individuals. She graded me as a four. Her evaluation was based on a comment I'd made many years ago while watching ER with her that

George Clooney was handsome. Was I maybe scoring a five now? I was sure that my earlier ogling of Shaloo's legs, this transformed person who was the very essence of all my fantasies of the beauty of the female form, must push me up one level at least.

"Trooper!"

Mother emerged from the elevator and waved to us, by the look of it high on schnapps and pills from the herbalist. I said good-bye to Shaloo and moved over to a couch in the corner of the bar.

"I'm on fire! God, this is going to be so much fun. I'm going to dance tonight, Trooper. That's for sure."

"Maybe you can take a turn with Mengele, back from the dead on the dance floor."

"Oh, come on! I've examined the ticket and there is no sign of Nazism. You're safe."

For a while she'd been quite nonchalant in the face of my cynicism towards the racists' ball, as her hash-jazz friend Tim Wallace had agreed to escort her. She'd even gone so far as to claim that she welcomed the chance to be rid of my nagging for one night, the constant preaching that would make even the most stoic person grind his teeth. She went on to say that in fact *I* was the only fascist, and so on and so forth. But then Tim was ordered to rest after kidney surgery and she was back to square one. So now she felt she had to be nice to me again. She pointed to the tray with the shot glasses and told me that it was very kind of me to make such an effort.

"Want some? Sex on the Beach, My Bloody Fucking Valentine, or just a good, old Brain Damage? Dmitri's been busy."

"No, not really. I think I'd rather just have a cold beer," she said as if it were the equivalent of joining a nunnery. "On such a nice day as this I sometimes enjoy a nice glass of beer. The only fault

I find with the hotel is that the fridge in the room should be a bit bigger, you know, for the beer."

"I just keep it in my belly."

She pointed out that not everyone wished to look like a pit bull and then quoted Great Aunt Edda, who'd said that it was better to stick to spirits if one wanted to lose weight. In that sense Brain Damage was ideal. We made a toast and Mother slapped the tickets to the Nazi ball on the table, along with a flyer for the Icelandic bank party. She felt it was incredible that two such grand events should be planned on the same day and in the same building.

"I'm determined to drop in on the bank party first," she said. "I suppose it was nice getting that bottle of champagne the other day, but really, what is that compared to all those billions?"

"We're not going to go there to hoard wine, Mother." I had a bad feeling about this. If Mother had decided to drink her share of the Icelandic banking profits in one afternoon, I was in for a nightmare of an evening.

"So now you're going to forbid me to go to the bankers' party?"

"No, but you're going on your own. I'm not setting foot in there."

"Is there no end to your tediousness, Hermann? It's pathological." She stared into her beer and kept silent as if she was pondering how best to tackle this problem. "I was so sure I'd meet a gentleman."

"I just can't do it, Eva. The last thing I want is to spend an evening with the Klambra boys on top of everything." When she pretended not to understand I reminded her that, before my life started revolving around drinking sessions and museum trips with her, I'd worked at the Klambra Real Estate Agency in Reykjavik. I'd read that the owners, father and son, had some dubious business dealings out here, and I was sure that Amsterdam was their city of choice so they could snoop around the holes of the IceSave bankers. There was no chance in hell I was going to show up at this gathering of necrophiliacs and risk running into them.

"Aren't you being overly negative like usual?" Mother asked and gave me a withering look. I felt the need to explain myself. My job at the real estate agency had taken up three years of my life, a period that spanned the most excessive period of hyperconsumerism in the history of Iceland. We made such a killing one month that the office closed for over a week while Benni, the father, had a Jacuzzi room installed. He insisted that this would "greatly increase our opportunities in the upper levels of the market," somehow believing that people who invested in luxury apartments would rather buy them from Klambra because Klambra had a hot tub—because people who had millions to spend on real estate in apartment buildings would relish the chance for a free bath. The true purpose of course, was to provide the Klambra boys with an R&R room where they could do their coke and whoring.

When I resigned because Zola and I were moving to Ireland they owed me over two million kronur for overtime, as it had been my lot to clean up the boys' fiascos. The money was supposed to pay for our room and board in Ireland, but Benni always had an excuse when I tried to collect my salary. He told me that his son Daniel was responsible for this stuff, there were a few things that needed clearing up first, he couldn't find my letter of resignation—was I sure I handed it in? He said that this needed to be 100% certain because of tax matters. Finally, the boys told me that I'd have to take them to court if I wanted to try and get paid for hours no one recalled me putting in, and everything around my resignation was very muddled and bore witness to my sloppy work ethics. I slammed the door when I left and shut those two million down in the deepest, blackest hole in my brain, where I kept all the darkest and nastiest stuff that my psyche had repressed during my life, and I promised myself to forget this along with everything else Klambra boys related.

"You know why I'm not jumping at the chance to join the bankers' party. I'll take you to frolic with the neo-Nazis, but that's it."

"I suppose I'll skip it too, since you feel so strongly about this. If I'd known they had behaved so abhorrently . . . I'm not even sure I would have accepted that champagne. That's one thing that can be said about the two of us, Trooper—we are not for sale."

"I'll drink to that," I said and asked for the bill. "Do you want me to ask him to call a cab?"

"No, Ramjiminn will drive us to the ball."

"Why would you involve him in this? I thought he had the night off."

"Sure, but this is not just any night, Trooper. It's not as if the two of us do this every night—dress up in our Sunday best and head out for adventure. He was very pleased to help."

Daylight was surrendering to dusk when Ramji arrived to pick us up in the Ambassador. The hubbub outside the conference hall indicated that there was even more going on than a Nazi ball and an Icelandic bankers' party. Ramji, with his uncanny ability to find parking where there was none, managed to squeeze the car between a hotdog stand and a garbage can. Suddenly he went chalk white.

"Mam BriemMam, I must hurry. I must say good-bye now."

"Is everything okay, Ramjiminn?"

"Everything is okay, EvaMam, but now I must go."

78

It was evident that something had upset the driver even though he seemed intent on hiding it. The mystery was solved in the next instant when a big man with a turban came rambling over and banged on the car window.

"Ramji," he bellowed, pushing down the window with strength fit for the circus. "If you want a proper job you come and talk to us Rotandaris. We can use more drivers. It is me, Bubi, you know me."

"Yes, sir," Ramji said. "But no thank you. I have a job."

"How about you?" the big man said, pointing to Mother and me. "Can you drive cars? Choppers?"

"Mister Bubi, sir," Ramji said and seemed to edge ever closer to the precipice of life as the man refused to leave. "Mam Briem needs to go to a ball, sir, and Mr. Willyson must join her. You have to let them go now."

"Who was that clown?" Mother asked when the man ambled off. "What on earth was that all about?"

"Mr. Bubi, Mam. My old boss. He is very determined."

"So am I, Ramjminn. I'm determined to go to the ball."

"You just go, Ramji. We'll catch a cab later."

He drove off and I ran to catch up with Eva, who had managed to mow down the people waiting in line to get into the Nazi ball. I only just managed to grab her sleeve before she disappeared inside with both our tickets. Heading over to the bar, I came across a brutishly ugly, mustachioed male exchanging bad breath with a female of the same species, an ambiguous cross between human and hippopotamus. The male had inked something vague but slightly familiar on his forehead . . . Could it really be? The hope of confirming the truth raced through my soul. I greeted the couple and could not take my eyes off the tattoo on the man's forehead. The opportunity was too good to resist.

"This is Hans, our brother in Christ," I said, introducing the creature to Mother. "I'm not going to detain you from your friends for too long, Hans, but it is always a pleasure to meet a brother in Christ and I wanted you to meet my mother."

"Eva Briem," Mother said, oblivious to where I was going with this until she noticed the tattoo and shot me a look.

"My pleasure," Hans replied. "It truly is my pleasure to meet a brother and sister in Christ. May the Lord be with you and bring us together again. Hallelujah!"

"Did you see that?" I roared with laughter when the bull was out of earshot. "Did you see the fucking swastika *tattooed* on his *forehead?*"

"It was obviously old. Very, very faint."

"As if that changes anything. These creeps don't change overnight just because they join a cult. They're hateful people and always will be. I told you this was a racist gathering. I. TOLD. YOU. SO."

To make up for my little victory I promised to get Mother another Campari. She agreed to forgive me only if I promised to be wholeheartedly entertaining for the rest of the evening, which I did. But then my worst fears came true: there was an exodus from the bankers' party over to the Nazi ball. The Klambra boys had taken over a leather couch a short distance from our table. Benni was cackling at his own jokes and Daniel sat stone-faced with his featherbrain engaged in some inner dimensions of kinky sex and insider trading. They sat there with their coke-fueled laughter, their tumblers of century-old single malt whiskey mixed with cola, and Cuban cigars, having the time of their lives at the Nazi ball with Mother and me. All the dark and repressed memories that I'd buried in the graveyard of my brain now clawed their way back to the surface. Benni stared at me, with no apparent recollection of owing me a thing, because he shot out of his seat and shouted across the room: "Hermann! Fucking hell! It's the fucking Herminator!"

"Good evening, Benni."

"What the hell, man! You in the loop?"

"No, Benni. I'm not in the *loop*," I answered and was suddenly thrilled to be with my mother at a Nazi ball. "I'm here with my mother, just having a good time. Brain Damage and herbs, it's *da bomb*."

"Weren't you at the meeting with Sjonni? Here for the greens? The Ice Baron takes care of his peeps, man. Fixrenta is taking over the buy-to-travel market. It's genius, Hermann. Pure genius!"

"Now you listen to me," Mother said. She found Benni revolting and hated him intensely after my tale of the two million. "We're here to have a good time, or are at least trying to, but you're not making it easy. I have cancer and Trooper and I are here so I can kill myself. But first I just wanted to have a bit of fun, so please crawl back into whatever hole you came out of."

Benni took a few steps backward. "See you around, Hermann, my man. Peace out."

"What happened to that cash you owe me?" I called, because my hatred was back from the dead, putrid and vengeful.

"Sorry?"

"My salary that you held back, the two million?"

"What? You're still on about that shit? It's in the past, Hermann, let it be. Danni and I are really onto something in Bulgaria these days, you should come too. It's got everything—huge bonuses . . . you should check it out. We're not talking millions, my man, *we're talking billions*." I got the feeling this phrase was being used a lot at Klambra office these days. "So is the Herminator hot for some greens?"

"What are these greens you're going on about?" Mother interjected. "Is the idiocy in Iceland now at such a level that even businessmen can't speak Icelandic anymore?"

"No, Benni," I said, wanting to put an end to this. "I don't think I'll buy into Bulgaria. Illness and all. It's taxing."

"Yes, of course," Benni said, as if Mother's madness was suddenly understandable in light of her cancer. I remembered that his father, the don of the Klambra boys, had kicked it because of a tumor a few years back, and how Benni and Daniel had needed several strippers to help them mourn. "Hang on, Hermann, I'll have a word with Danni. Maybe he can find a solution to this. We have a nice apartment here in the 'burbs."

"Shit," I said and looked at Mother, who shook her head and then her glass, indicating that she needed a refill on her Campari to survive. But surviving would have to wait because Daniel was on his feet in his tight suit, sunglasses and a shit-eating grin that suggested a life of extreme dental care; a deluxe, updated model of Benni.

"Ach," Mother said, recoiling. "Is that the son?"

"Huuur-MAN!" he said and squeezed between us. "Waaassaaap? Douwn widdah mon-nay?" The phrases sounded like Japanese to me, waa-saap, wid-dah, mon-nay. As it turned out, after a few more phrases, I had been right: the boys were in Amsterdam to beg. The Icelandic holding company, Fixrenta, formerly known as Klambra Group, had secured a loan for a few billion from the bankers with the champagne. The boys really were in the loop, had hit the jackpot so to speak, and were going to use the money to build golf condos in Bulgaria. They had also bought a four-story building in Herengracht, which was to house Fixrenta's HQ in Europe and a couple apartments. I should drop in for some *Veuve Clic*—the place was always full of *honeys*.

Daniel's presence and his motor mouth seemed to be driving Mother off the deep end; she was tense enough from having to wait for her drink. I decided it was best to agree to everything he said, so I pretended to accept his offer and thanked him. Told him we'd be in touch. Clumsy *gangsta*-handshake.

"What a creepy man," Mother said when he was gone. "Fidgeting about like that and going on and on about himself without so much as offering a lady a drink."

"I'll take care of it. I'll get us something strong from the bar."

When I returned with a selection of tequila shots, one of the racists had taken a seat next to Mother and seemed to be admiring her earlobes. I found it perverse that a man would try to pick up elderly ladies by complimenting their earlobes and quickly drove him away. It was time to call it a night. We downed the shots, stood up and walked out into the night. A polka-dotted Amsterdam shimmered under the summer sky, the artificially lit darkness ready to gobble up the day and pave the way for the underworld. People shouted profanities at lampposts and threw beer cans, the atmosphere was intoxicated, and there was no Ramji to lead the way. I was about to chase down a cab when the bulky Indian with the turban came running, grabbed me, and stared at me with eyes full of spite.

"I saw where you were," he shouted. "I saw where you are coming from. Racists!"

I couldn't say anything. After all, I had just come from a gathering of racists.

"You people are a plague on the planet, you are human feces. Feces!

He let go of me and walked off.

"What a brute," Mother said, insulted by this outburst. "What on earth was he thinking?"

"It's what happens when you go to a Nazi ball. It's time to go home."

We caught a cab to the hotel, where I made us a long drink while she laid out her tarot cards. She was sorry to tell me that the chances of me finding a woman in the near future were very slim indeed and that I should expect hard times financially as the year wore on. Things looked good in the long run, though.

"But now it's my turn," she said and lit up as she always did when expecting a prophesy. "I'm sure that my luck is about to change for the better."

She picked nine cards from the deck and they were all as expected: some difficulties, then tranquility, stability, new feelings and finally . . .

"There he is again!"

"Who?"

"The knight, of course!" Excited, she stuck the card in my face. A regal looking man in a kilt riding across clouds under a golden sunset. "What does this mean, Trooper? Will I meet the knight in the kilt?"

Chapter
9

I couldn't help but wonder now and again whether our trip was something more than one big question about the quintessential issues: a whole tarot tournament on life, death, and love, and whether the answer in the end would be anything more than a hollow, intangible sound fading into silence. The fact was that I would in all probability have many decades to ponder the so-called big questions, half a lifetime left for anxiety, nostalgia, and self-doubt, while life was slipping further away from Mother with each passing day.

The absoluteness of this fact hit me now and again like cold slush to the face. I suppose all journeys are melancholy because they encapsulate things that can never be repeated, but my trip with Mother was especially so: a rambling journey to the end of the line. When we weren't strolling alongside the canals or relaxing slightly tipsy at the hotel—Mother on her balcony with her newly developed yoga program and me in my room, engulfed in the possibilities of the TV remote—I would often think about how lonely she must be, and how harsh it was to have to face Death and watch him rob you of all that never came to be.

Deep down I was unsure that she would get better on Dr. Fred's Ukrain. The reason was not only that medical science had given us other options, but also that the odds were against us. We hadn't come all this way to ensure the progression of life, but death was just one of the many possibilities framing our journey, not a player in our revelry. Mother was here because she had no other choice and I was simply here to do the impossible: to make her happy for the last days of her life.

I was haunted on a regular basis by self-doubt regarding the task. I suspected that however hard I tried, the adventure would never fully be realized while we spent our days aimlessly roaming the city. We drank our morning cup of coffee on the balcony and visited museums and galleries before returning to the hotel to continue our session of specials from the night before. Mother sang Nina Simone songs and told anecdotes of drives in the country and a lost bottle of booze in the woods. Stories from the past became stories of the near future.

But no matter how well I performed I was never more than a stand-in for the guy who's role this should have been. The obvious fact was that Mother needed a lover. Despite an operatic temperament and extraordinary physical strength, she had always been a vulnerable woman and longed to rest in the arms of someone stronger. This had always puzzled me, especially given her incredibly firm opinions on how I lived my own life. She had waited for the solution for years, something that would finally bring her to smooth sailing.

Where this deep longing came from, I didn't know. Through the years she had blossomed in various parallel dimensions, marriages to deans, socializing with royalty, and an intimate friendship with the Danish TV characters, Nikolaj and Julie, whom she met every now and again according to this alternative reality in the restaurant Skindbuksen in Copenhagen along with her husband, Peter Toft Jensen. It was enough to see Mother at karaoke in her dancing shoes to realize that her dreams were a stark contrast to what really made her happy. But that had no effect on the conclusion: she wanted a man. I'd dreaded this from the beginning and hoped that the issue would be resolved without my help. That we'd meet some former headmaster at a gallery, preferably also suffering from some terminal disease and, after that, Mother would float along on her happy cloud while I'd try some hunting of my own in the bars, like a lion in the jungle of love. But that was not in the cards. Managing the drugs and their effects and nuances was child's play compared to the impenetrable wall that I now faced, to help Mother fall in love for the last time. I finally decided to send in a personal ad to three respectable cultural publications: *Opera Nieuws*, *Bibliotheek en Boekhandelaar*, and an evening paper that allegedly no one but old socialists picked up. The ad read:

> *Elegant woman in early sixties looking for gentleman of similar age for conversation, dining, museums, theater & concerts. Reply in English with <u>photo</u> and phone no. P.O. Box 3149 in main post office Radhuisstraat & Singel bf. June 1st.*

I felt it was necessary to underline the word "photo" because Mother was vain when it came to the looks of her lovers. She loathed short men and spoke in condescending tones about those who'd fallen like single socks out of washing machines. She would go into graphic detail when describing the various physical qualities she admired in men: broad shoulders, strong features, and a Buddha-belly. She had an aversion to thin men and felt the same way about the obese. She didn't mind if a man wasn't handsome as long as he had enough charm to make up for it. Certain primitiveness in the facial features could flatter a man if the eyes radiated intelligence and the jawline suggested daring. She despised sentimental types, but appreciated kindness. In fact, Mother didn't want a man, she wanted a he-male, and she was ready to forgive the most severe personality flaws, such as serious drinking problems and insanity, if men had that certain masculinity she desired. This had more often than not been her downfall, and I was determined to keep the swashbuckling drunks at bay. The choice of the he-male was most important of all, the final brush stroke in this work of art.

I was quite excited when I finally ventured out into the summer heat the first day of June with my course set for the post office. Over forty responses tumbled out of the post box, and I found nineteen of them interesting enough to make up a little pile for me to examine at length. Of those nineteen applicants, twelve got bonus points for wit, extraordinary good looks, or a lovely turn of phrase. I sorted the letters by quality and called the eligible ones. Most of them thought it strange that Mother didn't call them herself and refused to speak to me. I asked the others to give me a chance. I explained that Mother was an intelligent and interesting woman who'd had to go abroad on short notice. She would very much appreciate it if the prospective gentleman would meet with me, her son, for a quick chat at Café Cutty Sark on Spuistraat before she got back to the country.

The elite six were all retired and agreed to meet me, one after the other, on a rain-splashed Tuesday in the beginning of July. I found a quiet table in the corner half an hour before the first meeting, completely unaware of the torture awaiting me. I had never seen such pathetic specimens of the human race as the miserable lot who found their way into Café Cutty Sark that dreary afternoon. I thought I'd found my man in John Devanugh, a handsome type with great bone structure and an interest in dramaturgy until I realized that his "recently deceased" wife had actually been dead for twenty years. We didn't have time for this shit. I knew that Mother would have no patience or tolerance for some long-dead female who was apparently superior to any living human. I said good-bye to John Devanugh and hello to Stefan Sauerbritzl, a German and compulsive eater who was either freakishly photogenic or a master at Photoshop. The meetings deteriorated from then on. Ben Henderson, real estate agent, a malodorous bearded ape with skin problems. Valmer Flint was a pervert. Then there was the incorrigible alcoholic from Rotterdam, and a lethargic Finn with transgender fantasies. In short, these meetings all proved the point that Mother had been making for years about single men over fifty.

"No luck?" the waitress smiled as she wiped my table clean. I wanted to take off with her to Casablanca and disappear into the intoxicating infinity of her youth. "No one fit the part? I mean, aren't you making a movie?"

"Yes. No. I'm just looking for a man who's ready for a romantic relationship. It's hard to find the right kind at this age."

"Don't you have to try for guys a bit younger?" the girl asked, slightly surprised.

"Younger men are all busy with other things. And Mother . . . no, it wouldn't work."

"Is she really difficult?"

"No, she's fine. I wouldn't go through all this trouble otherwise."

"Then you're lucky. My friend doesn't dare come out because his mom is such a bitch."

"I have the exact opposite problem, she's always trying to drag me out. And then it always ends with the tarot cards."

"She sounds really supportive. And what do the cards say? A loverman in the cards at all?"

"I was hoping to seal the deal today," I sighed. "You saw how it went. It's true what they say—love is more complicated after fifty."

"You should check out the service just up the street," she suggested and poured me another coffee. "It's called Hemingway something . . . Dating Service."

"Hemingway Dating Service? Is it for Hemingways or with Hemingways?"

"With Hemingways. I'm sure you'll find Mr. Right before you know it."

I thanked her, left the café and walked farther up the street. The Hemingway Dating Service was at number 224, in a very narrow building that opened up once you got inside, like the first floor had spread into the neighboring houses. There were ladies in heavy coats whose potent smell conjured up the fear of dead animals. I was reminded of my youth. Surrounded by a fantastic horniness that simmered underneath the polished surface, I walked over to the front desk and fished out a form from a plastic box.

"You're seeking a man in his sixties?" the receptionist asked when I handed her the paper.

"With an interest in literature, theater and such. Handsome."

She picked up the phone and then pointed me to the bar next door, where I was about to rock Mother's gay-scale. There, I had a passionate conversation with an intelligent man named Radberth

Comstock, an engineer at the Academy of Science, classy in a shirt and blue jeans with tartan-laced pockets. Here was the Highland knight himself in a gilded sunset, and I had become my mother.

"There's been a misunderstanding," I said as it finally dawned on me.

The rain soaked parking lot steamed under my feet as I stormed back into Hemingway Dating Service, ready to prove to the world that Hermann Willyson was a ladies' man. Would the reception-ist like a drink? I was great company, a true he-male who'd simply come to fill out a form for his mother.

"I suppose I owe you one. I'll go over the listings with you if you can wait a couple."

We ran down Spuistraat in the rain and found shelter under a blue canvas. Me and Gloria Birkenstock, matchmaker and the focus of my sex drive. Fortunately, the beer had the intended numbing effect on my nervous system and I told her stories and bad jokes about racecar games and salmon fishing, digging up all the pitiful machismo I could muster to breathe in the estrogen in Gloria. I drank like my life depended on it.

"I suppose I should've known," she laughed.

"All that matters is that I'm here with you, Gloria. This is the life, Gloria. This is the *life*."

"Cheers to that!"

"And cheers to Radberth Comstock. He'll make some lucky guy very happy."

We sat at the pub for a couple of hours without so much as a glance at the listings. I told her about Mother's illness and our trip to Lowland. We found that we had the same birthday, nine years apart. She possessed a joyful sex appeal that conjured up youthful tension. As I lay naked next to her shortly after leaving the café, I was haunted by an onslaught of thoughts: why am I not sleeping with a woman I love instead of lying here with a stranger? Why am I hiding my paunch belly and genitals with a stuffed animal? Why do I choose to have sex with a woman who has the same last name as my sandals? I hadn't had sex with a woman since the beast with the bearded tits had her way with me in Dublin. After that I developed a sexual inferiority complex, which grew in proportion to my bloated self. In the heat of the moment the feeling had disappeared, but now it returned with a vengeance. Gloria Birkenstock was a beautiful woman, long-legged and slight, with full, round breasts that reminded me of two halves of an Olympic size handball. She was a woman any man would be proud to share his bed with. Nevertheless, I found it impossible to relax beside her and soon stood up to call Ramji.

"Do you mind if I ride along?" she asked when I told the driver to take me back to the hotel. "I feel like going for a stroll and the walk back would be perfect."

I told her I needed to stop by Pijlsteeg and that the driver had strict orders to take me to get some cannabis. Gloria was unconcerned and told me she didn't care where we were headed. When we got to the museum I felt obliged to invite her in with me to where the doctor's son sat smoking in his underwear. Only a couple hours had passed since my premature ejaculation had ended its journey in Gloria's latex-filled cervix, but what happened next was beyond past events. Steven looked at Gloria and Gloria looked at Steven. She was twelve years his senior; he wanted a lover who would give him a motherly sense of security. Most normal people would perhaps have taken offence to this turn of events, but I had trouble containing my joy. After telling them a few jokes about Gaddafi, president of Libya, I bid a warm farewell to the couple with numerous hand-shakes and expressions of hope to meet again soon.

Once out in the street I was gripped by a pure desire to fulfill my ideas from that morning: find a sleazy dive and start a marathon session of special drinks. Ramji seemed to sense the self-destructive impulse in me and refused to leave me alone. We sat for a good half hour at Blue Blue Jay Jay, a soft-core topless joint where I downed margaritas and Ramji sipped on his mineral water until he insisted on leaving, appalled by his client's taste in watering holes. I tried to explain to him that we were equals and that I was very fond of him, and if something offended him he should say so.

"Yes, sir," he said and drove me to Nieuwenmarkt, the very heart of prostitution and drug dealing in the city. "I don't think you should go there, Mr. Trooper."

I had hardly gotten out of the car when I was back in trouble, entranced by Steven's super-joint. A stout man on a motorbike with the words "Rent your own Taxi from Rotandari Taxi" plastered on the side rolled menacingly toward me. I automatically grabbed a piece of patio furniture leaning against a nearby wall and hit him with it. The big man hardly flinched, got off his bike, took off his helmet, and sunk his powerful fist into my left jaw.

"Racist!" he yelled, pulling back his arm, ready to strike again. "I saw you at that racist gathering! Colonial cunt!"

He put me in a headlock, twisted my arms behind my back and ground my face into the sidewalk. I saw broken glass and gobs of gum, and the lowest parts of passersby: tights and shoes that whisked past without stopping, without any interference, because people were used to violence and fighting, endless hate and abuse. I screamed that it hurt.

"And for the Indians who live in little rooms far away from the city to wake up and drive Dutch Daisies to restaurants, and then just get spit on, you think it doesn't hurt?"

"I'm not Dutch!" I almost cried. The pain was starting to cut through the numbness of the weed and I was beaten up and humiliated by Bubi Rotandari the taxi driver. "I'm from Iceland!"

Of all the things I could have said, but didn't get to say to Bubi Rotandari at that moment, about my political correctness, my love for the multicultural and orgies with whites, Indians, and Masai—with all due respect for the cultural uniqueness of peoples such as the Sikhs—this declaration of my nationality seemed to be my get-out-of-jail card this time.

"Iceland? So you know Binu Singh Fagandi, my uncle. Hmm. Come with me."

According to information related by Binu Singh Fagandi, Icelanders were a remarkable exception in the world of the White West, which had royally fucked up with Mr. Bush at the helm. President Bush had made money for his war by selling luxury apartments in Hollywood, but now there were no buyers so Mr. President Bush was poor. Icelanders, however, were not poor because they owned a bank in the Netherlands. Bubi had seen the bankers himself at a party next to a racist gathering. Icelanders were world champions in money making.

How all this tied in with his plans for me, I had no idea, but I was by no means a free man yet. My half-hearted attempt to get up reawakened his fist.

"Mr. Bubi, sir," Ramji called out, having parked the car to try and talk sense into his old boss. "I saw what happened, sir. I think that even though Mr. Willyson was careless, sir, I don't think he hit you on purpose. It was an accident, Mr. Bubi, that's all."

94

"You swear it, Ramji? Can you swear it on our Punjabi ancestors?"

"I swear it, Mr. Bubi, this is the truth. Mr. Hermann Willyson made an accident."

"Ok. I do this for my father, Ramji, I do this because you are family and because my father is a good man who takes care of his people. As do I. You can go. But when I want to collect my debt from Mr. Willyson—it is dishonorable to hit someone with garden furniture—I will call you, Ramji. This will do for now. Mr. Willyson is free to go." He was about to stand up when he suddenly turned around, stared at me intently and said: "One more thing, Mr. Hermann Willyson. Does your name mean 'brother,' like in Spanish?"

"No, it doesn't mean brother. I suppose it means soldier. I think so: soldier."

"Mr. Soldier? Mr. Soldier, very good. Mr. Soldier is dismissed."

We walked back to the Ambassador and got in. I stared vacantly out of the window at the endless, red-eyed traffic slithering by. I felt a steady beat at my temples and a growing sense of nausea punctuated by bursts of needing to drown it in liquor and junk food. When I finally made it back to the hotel I was in no mood to face what had happened sober, so I ambushed the minibar with inspired grandeur, took two painkillers and barreled down to the restaurant to order a Bloody Mary and a large helping of French fries with mayo. My friend Dmitri watched bemused as I wolfed down my food and drink, and topped up my glass on the house. The relief over not feeling horrible swept away what little remained of any common sense in my being. I walked out of the lobby, light as a feather, knowing the only way I'd go to sleep was if I passed out. It's hard to accurately assess the time, but I vaguely recall the growing gray light when I crawled out at dawn from some doomed hash dive in the Red Light District, a good twenty hours after I'd walked with great expectations down Spuistraat in search of the perfect he-male.

"Trooper, my lovely boy!" Mother sat at the hotel bar with the latest issue of *Bild*. "Now, you go lie down and get a good, long rest, like a babe in a cradle. *Mutti* will take care of her little super trooper, and everything will be just the way it used to be."

I dozed off with childhood lullabies ringing in my ears, drifting off into fits of dreamless sleep.

Chapter
10

After my run-in with Bubi I mostly kept to myself. I slept until
noon, had a latté on the balcony, read, called Helena, and checked
in on Mother every now and again. In the evenings we took the
elevator down to the restaurant or found a small pub nearby where
we could have a bite and something to drink. I spiked her gin with
calamus—a wonder drug from the Smart-Shop in Warmoesstrat
that obviously did what it said on the label. Two glasses of Gordon's
with calamus set Mother on fire. She laughed and sang sappy songs
about the student life and drinking wine, like a slushed recording
of her thirty-years-younger self. Her face lit up with exaggerated
delight and she threw her head back in laughter, whipped her high-
heeled feet up on the table and shouted for more jenever—let's
drink! I kept them coming like a factory worker, either helplessly
inebriated, or shattered by a hangover. If I suggested that we'd leave
early she accused me of being Hrafn Gunnlaugsson, an Icelandic
filmmaker she abhorred. "It's only one o'clock, Trooper! More jenever!" Then she'd launch into a repertoire of socialist songs from
days of yore. The music poured into my soul like a melancholy
porridge of stress and happiness. The rhythm reminded me of the
heavy rains in the Reykjavik of my youth, a deep drumming of

incoming low pressure from the Atlantic. I didn't sing along, but let my mind drift into the din and song, until Mother realized I was dozing off and sent me to the bar for more.

This was one of the things I'd completely forgotten to take into account when we set sail for the Netherlands: the daily, almost incessant partying was conjuring up a potent alcoholism in me. Like many others, I enjoyed babbling nonsense and drowning the world's sorrows in drink, but despite having earned my stripes in sherry marathons on Spítala Street I had never possessed Mother's stamina for the merciless binges she dragged me on during our stay at Hotel Europa. I was sucked into a world where the laws were alien and stronger than I was, and all I could do was go with the flow and try to contain the rising anxiety looming behind the conviction that I wasn't in control of anything at all. Mid-day took me out on the balcony with a glass of red and a bong while the hubbub of the day evaporated into the stillness. I spent several days doing nothing but wandering around the hotel room in my underwear, reading books, doing crosswords, and having the only sex available for free: masturbation. The only time I ventured into daylight was when I needed provisions—Campari, cannabis, or new records for the gramophone.

On Saturdays I went to the market on Waterlooplein to rummage through endless stacks of vinyl, amazed at finding albums I thought were unobtainable, but were actually hidden like buried gold among all the junk. There was the New Wave and Indie Pop that Zola had collected on her numerous trips to Ireland and which she insisted I take after we broke up. The Stone Roses, New Order, Sonic Youth. I'd adopted her musical tastes in the first months of our relationship. We'd lie on her sofa and listen to the records that I felt spoke to me in the same way that Zola did, like an exotic, irresistible voice from a world that seemed to only grow and expand. When Zola left and told me to keep the records because she had no room for them, I took it as one more nail in this cruel and incomprehensible coffin of rejection: that even the memories of the past, the most beautiful thing we had, was a dimension she no longer wanted to know. Had Zola disappeared into the void? I was warped by bitterness that instantly melted into sorrow, like a rag in an oversized tumble-dryer. Or was this maybe her way of communicating what she couldn't say: that she was sorry how things turned out, despite her incomprehensible behavior? And that maybe, one of these nights when I was looking through my records and time had sanded down all the things that went wrong, she would pick up the phone and say: *Sorry, Trooper, I understand what happened, I understand now that I was wrong.* She would fly to me from wherever she was and bittersweet music would fill the cosmos, the soft down on Zola's body . . .

"You buying those?" The record dealer whisked me back to the present and I realized how low I had sunk. I suppose there was no denying that I'd missed Zola terribly after the breakup and wanted to gut that French dentist of hers, but the fact of the matter was that she'd irritated me in so many ways while we were together. Peculiar interests like Gaelic funeral songs and ballet could drive the happiest of fools to suicidal thoughts. I had to remind myself that I was responsible in part for our dwindling sex life, choosing to spend my weekends with Dave, an annoying friend of ours on Grafton Street, drinking crème de menthe over soccer games. After I handed the record dealer 5 euros I imagined the Frenchman puking at the ballet, with a migraine due to Zola's incessant nagging about folk music. I longed for some sort of Iberian ham I'd tasted at a tapas bar in Galicia a long time ago. As I absentmindedly took up my crossword puzzle in a nearby pub I heard someone address me by name. Right next to me sat a woman who was looked exactly like Gloria the matchmaker, and it took me a second to realize it was in fact her.

"Trooper?" she asked and planted a motherly kiss on my lips. She was wearing a green tunic over tight, black pants, with a judo belt tied around her waist, and I simultaneously wanted to run away and to have passionate sex with her. "We're engaged," she said, glancing over at Steven, who I now noticed sitting at the table. "It's insane, of course, we know. But Trooper, neither one of us has done anything this *fun*, ever."

They kissed and we ordered a bottle of champagne, talked about the Euro Cup in Soccer, Rastafarism, and the upcoming wedding. Steven wanted to have a Jamaican reggae band called Satiricon. I was sure that the union of this unlikely couple had to be the best thing that had come out of my ramblings around Amsterdam. Aside from Helena, these two were the only people I could, without dramatic polarization, call my friends here in the city. Steven was so saturated by agoramanic innocence that Gloria hugged him in her delight. Until now I had always equated positivity of this scale with stupidity, but now I put that idea to rest. Meeting them by chance was a sign that there was something more than ethanol and oxygen encompassing my and Mother's existence here. After two hours of slurred happiness I said good-bye at the corner of Herengrach and walked back to the hotel with an ounce of tar-black hashish in my pocket.

"You smoking half-naked out there? It's not even noon!" Mother had seen me go out on the balcony and stood calamus-content in the doorway.

"It's actually past three," I said, "and I've been out and about since this morning. I met Steven, who gave me this as a parting gift."

"Well, then you might as well give it to me," she said and took the pipe, inhaled, and sat down opposite me. Her little trip to the Hash-Jazz, along with a few dedicated practice sessions in the various coffee shops, had given her a tolerance for the drug that was even greater than her superior stamina for drink. She chattered on about cousin Matti's hopeless experiments in growing tomatoes, and the degenerate indulgences of Caligula. She asked me if I'd read *I, Claudius*.

"Sorry?"

"*I, Claudius*. You know the book. Come on, are you completely dense, Trooper?"

"What are you talking about?"

"The book! An incredible story about the Roman Empire. I'm seriously amazed sometimes by your ignorance. And you're supposed to be my son."

"Supposed to be? Are you going to denounce me because I haven't read a book?"

"Hardly. We just have to accept that there is a certain injustice of the given."

Incidents like this were proof that Willy Nellyson and his big cock had not necessarily provided me with the intellect that ran in her side of the family. The fact that I had a magnetic memory that stubbornly held on to every little bit of information within its force field was of no significance. If I didn't know something she knew, she took it as a sign of the decline of civilization, the dumbing down of the generations raised on *Beverly-Hills*-something and *ER*. Time and again she would fish for some a random quote from the labyrinth of her mind and ask me: "You must know Britten. Don't you know who Cornelis Vreeswijk is? Goodness, you *are* ignorant." It was like being on Jeopardy twenty-four-seven.

I stood up, went inside, and turned on the TV. There was a program on young models in the United States. The girls were goddesses and their proclamations perfect for convincing Mother that there actually were people dumber than me.

"I think I would do anything to get ahead in the model business," Alice said and I translated for Mother: *I don't mind whoring and doing coke.* Francis had this to say about Alice: "She's charming, but she needs to work on her legs." *She's not just boring, she also walks like a duck.* "It's fantastic working with Damien," Dorothy said, "He's really good at bringing out the best in me!" *I'm so sexy! Everyone wants to fuck me!*

Mother wasn't interested so I changed the channel and found *Ten Years Younger*, a monstrous show about lost youth and beauty. Janine, a beige housewife from Essex, England, had aged more than ten years due to obsessive dieting and numerous pregnancies; now she'd had a thigh-tuck to prop up her ass, her teeth swapped out for a set of porcelains, and every strand of pubic hair burned off with a laser.

"It's such a blessing to be naturally beautiful," Mother said, "just think of all the trouble and pain people go through for looks. Just to look normal, really. Or would you say that woman is beautiful now? If you compare her to me, for instance?"

"Compared to you, Eva, Janine hasn't got a chance . . . but there's nothing *normal* about plastic dolls in their fifties. It's all hemorrhoids and smoker's cough."

Mother told me I was being vulgar and probably overdosing; she tended to outlast me anyway. She would sit there on the hotel balcony like the Sphinx of the desert and recite some irresistible wisdom from the depths of her soul while I whittled away into the matrix of cosmic fantasies or collapsed by the toilet bowl, dead pale and paranoid. I made the same mistake over and over again: thinking I could keep up with her. She claimed that the cannabis calmed her and made her lighter, like Oprah Winfred. It was plain to see that it had a very different effect on me.

"I think you should leave the stuff alone, Hermann, you don't have the stomach for it."

"You're not the only one who needs to relax."

"Have it your way, son. If your idea of relaxing is to hang out with your head in the toilet, then I'll have to leave you to it."

We went to bed early that evening. I turned on my side and fell asleep with my face squashed between the two mattresses of my king-size bed.

Chapter
11

W eekly visits to the doctor revealed that the treatment was working. Frederik didn't want to say too much about the progno-
sis, but did say the disease was not progressing. We had taken his
advice about enjoying life and followed his instructions to the letter
regarding the injections, never missing a shot. In fact, we were so
settled into our routine that I was slightly concerned when the doctor called me one morning in the middle of June to tell me that
Ramji was on his way to pick us up. There had been developments
with Eva's cancer and some news about the center. I got the sense
it was good news, but I wasn't at ease until we walked up the stairs
to the doctor's office. Dr. Fred smiled from ear to ear and gave us
a hearty welcome.

"Ukrain, you see, seems to either work quickly in people, or not
at all. We can usually tell in the second week or so. I like to give it
a bit more time before I discuss the effects with the patient, and it
pleases me to tell you, Mrs. Briem, that we are on the right track."

"It's all thanks to Trooper," Mother said, "and yourself, of course,
my dear Frederik. If I'd had my way, I would've let the jenever do
and left the Ukrain to the seriously ill. I've never felt really sick and
thought the injections were a bit frivolous. But I suppose I wouldn't

be here now if I hadn't listened to the two of you. Do you really believe this will make me better?"

"We'll have to wait and see, Mrs. Briem. You're in much better shape now than when we first met in April. There's a lot to celebrate. Did you see the crowd out on the lawn? This is a big day for you, Mrs. Briem, and a big day for Lowland. We have received a generous gift, a very generous gift indeed."

It was obvious that the doctor was touched. For a moment we stood as if nailed to the spot.

"One million euros is a lot of money for a hospice. I'm not very financially savvy but I do realize the significance of this. The donation will be put into a safe account, the interest from which should provide for Lowland longer than I'll be around."

"Congratulations," Mother said, squeezing the doctor's hand. "What wonderful news. Who is this great benefactor, if I may ask?"

"You may not, because it's a secret," answered the doctor. "Humble are the great at heart, as they say."

"And ill at heart are the mean and miserly," Mother replied. "I think we should walk out into the sun, my dear Frederik, and see what's going on out on the lawn."

A happy reunion took place soon as we were outside. Timothy Wallace from Missouri, Mother's friend from the Hash-Jazz, sat on a bench next to the fountain in his tank top with a cowboy hat and pipe. They had met a few times since spring and steadily became close friends. Each moment with Tim was like getting the world on an interest-free loan. He was sincere in his sarcasm, steadfast in his weaknesses, preferred the spiritual to the physical, and often spoke ill of the States, which Mother found to be a magnificent quality in an American. Mother thoroughly enjoyed sharing a joint with Tim and engaging in conversation that brought you momentarily closer to life. She wondered if they ever felt like this, these self-jetters who went to Italy to shop. She didn't need a self-jet for soul searching. She had Tim. He might not be a he-male in the sense of romantic love, but that didn't matter. She even let his bisexuality pass.

"Mamma!" he called to her in Icelandic and walked over to us smiling. I was blown away that he got away with calling her Mom. It was some sort of miracle. A dying woman in her sixties had had a second child.

"Happy birthday, Mountain Mama."

"It's Mountain Lady," Mother corrected him, referring to the poetic female incarnation of Iceland. "Mountain Lady—*Fjallkona*."

"All grown up now, *fjallkona*?"

"Yes I am," she answered. "Sixty-four today, like the republic. The 17th of June means rain in Reykjavik, but in Lowland we'll have life, Timothy. We have the sun. I'm told I am to live longer than the oldest of ancients, so if there ever was an occasion to have a smoke it has to be now."

He threw an arm over each of our shoulders and led us to a hollow out on the lawn. Garden furniture had been set up here and there for the occasion so visitors could have a seat and read about the center. A television crew from one of the stations was setting up to do a piece on the place, thanks to Helga's diligent work in the past days to promote the center's cause in the media. A donation of one million euros was good bait for publicity. She was going to formally open the event by holding a short speech in the restaurant pavilion, which was to open any minute.

"For the love of God, Trooper, go steal some beer for us. And a lemonade for Tim."

This was the only thing about Tim that Mother had needed some time to adjust to: he didn't drink. The explanation was that he used to drink incessantly, long ago when he was still married to his high school sweetheart, Gwinny. She turned out to prefer liquor undigested and, tired of cleaning up the vomit he left around the house, sent him to rehab. There he discovered the multiplicity of his sexual preferences, got divorced, founded a record company, made it big on Wall Street, and became a millionaire. Now he was dying and tried to make the most of his remaining time. "The very incarnation of the history of the United States," he would say. "That's why I'm trying to get this autobiography done before I kick the bucket."

"That's what I think you should do, Trooper. Since you're already keeping a journal. You can easily turn it into a biography. *Eva Briem Thórarinsdóttir and Life*. It would be a bestseller."

I decided to let them be and walked farther out on the lawn where a group of people had gathered around a small, gray-haired man in a white suit. My heart fluttered slightly, a common effect of celebrity on most people. The small man was none other than the palliative philosopher, Arthur van Österich, Helena's nemesis whom I'd seen at the Pleasure Fountain that spring. He was there to offer his thoughts on the center on this happy day.

Van Österich's imminent suicide was one of the hottest topics in the country at the time. The media speculated the method of choice: arsenic, the Atlantic, hypothermia on Mont Blanc? Would he allow a live broadcast on the European Broadcasting Union stations? The morning paper *De Telegraaf* reported his every move and published articles on developments in the Van Österich case. Van Österich bought socks in a sports store on Kalverstraat—did he intend to choke on a Speedo sock? Would he slit his wrists, as he had been seen buying a set of kitchen knives in Baden-Baden?

An article about Van Österich in the magazine *Gezondheid jaarlijks* caused much controversy by publishing a checklist for those set on taking their own lives. The magazine was accused of anti-life propaganda, but others praised the article for offering vital information on this moral issue. For it was not as easy as it might seem to put an end to your own life. There was the story of the man who was so intent on killing himself that he was a living testament to the tenacity of the human body and its inherent hatred of death. Freddy Borparter had tried every sure-fire method to halt the beating of his heart: he had swallowed pills, stuck his head in the oven, thrown himself off a cliff. But all his efforts got him was a mid-level position in a real estate agency.

The people out on the lawn had various opinions of Van Österich. Some loved him and thought it was terrible for the Netherlands to lose such a son. Others were more skeptical and some truly loathed him. What troubled most people was that he made no distinction between mental or physical pain when it came to the right of the individual to assisted suicide. Van Österich was not only an advocate of euthanasia as it was practiced in certain institutions, but was also a strong supporter of the idea that each human had the sole right to his/her life. In his opinion, suicide was a brave option out of the terrible abyss of depression.

"So get on with it, Van Österich! We're tired of waiting!" Someone shouted, and then a red water balloon smashed against the philosopher's chest, but he regained his composure in world-record time and carried on as if nothing had happened. The balloonist was grabbed by two strong men from the group of guests, and escorted off the property along with a few of his pals who were suspected of trying to cause more trouble.

"Isn't this just typical for the way things are in society these days, Van Österich?" a photographer from *De Telegraaf* asked. He had caught the attack on film. "I'm not trying to justify this sort of behavior—but don't you think that people are growing tired of this flirtation with death? What about those who are left behind? A friend of mine tried this."

I couldn't catch Van Österich's answer because it was drowned out by exclamations about a lack of beer. Mother had crept up on me and was talking wildly about a drought in the hollow. She went dead silent when she looked out on the lawn.

"Euch," she said. "Isn't that the Ostrich idiot over there?"

I had expected her to become irritated by the philosopher's presence. She'd heard that he was horrible. If his name came up in conversation she would always refer to him as the Ostrich, the Featherman, or even the Bird-Flu. She reveled in comments such as "his type like to stick their head in the sand, they should be plucking that bird, someone should clip his wings." I ignored this—we hardly knew the man. Ever since Helena pointed out his website to me, it had been my main source of information on assisted suicide, my guide through the maze of euthanasia. Mother, of course, had no clue.

As we got closer to the crowd and blended in with the media people and the guests, Mother's face reflected bitter disdain. The photographer from *De Telegraaf* seemed to feel the same and challenged the philosopher.

"I'll answer any comment," Van Österich said. "Take on any opposition against every person's right to suicide!"

To stop Mother from engaging in combat I offered myself up and started recounting the story of a school friend who had lived in constant fear of his father's self-destructive nature. His father gave weight to his threats of suicide by making actions speak for themselves: he bought arsenic, spent a fortune on rope, and carried the toaster into the bathroom when he took a bath, all to heighten the sensation of proximity to death. As a result my friend became a nervous wreck and refused to leave the house. I asked Van Österich if he didn't think it unfair and cruel for children to live in such fear.

"The idea is one thing and the implementation another," he answered. "People should not threaten suicide to manipulate others, especially not children."

"Yet that's how it is now with my friend," the photographer interjected and moved closer to me as if we were a team. "It's not easy dealing with people who are dead-set on killing themselves."

I tried to move away from the photographer, but to no avail. Van Österich spread out his arms and spoke to the two of us. "Family and friendship, if that sort of communication really exists without hypocrisy, must always be second to the individual's right to be or not to be. We can argue that a parent has duties toward a child, but to claim that this parent must live with suffering to spare the offspring discomfort is absurd."

"You call it discomfort for a child to lose its father?" a different man exclaimed in shock.

"Or for a friend to live in constant fear of the worst?" the photographer added. "It's hell."

"Really?" Van Österich asked. "Is that really the worst thing that could happen to you? That your friend decides to make good on his threats one day? Nobody decides to take his own life for revenge. These people are desperate. They live in constant darkness. Constant suffering. A true friend would not wish that kind of life for anyone."

"Go to Switzerland, Van Österich, we don't need people with your ideas in the Netherlands!" the shocked man shouted. He was wearing a T-shirt that read "Suicide is Sin." Van Österich said he had no need to go to Switzerland, there were plenty of people who agreed with him there. The photographer shook his fist and said that the philosopher obviously never had any friends. It was getting too heated for my taste and I wanted to get out of there. The intent had been to draw attention to the issue, but the event was on the verge of turning violent. The photographer wanted the philosopher to give a straight answer regarding his stance toward the dilemma of my school friend. Did he really believe that the father's suicide was justifiable?

"We have institutions that take care of orphaned children," Van Österich answered. "Support groups and adoption agencies. A person who can't get past their suffering, however, has no shelter except death."

"Strange how such a high-flyer can be such a dud," Mother whispered and leaned against me with a grimace. "Everything he says sounds like a recording."

"At least he's fighting in our corner," I said. "Defending what we'd do if things took a serious turn for the worse."

"Luckily we don't seem to have to worry about that, Trooper. And I have no wish to say good-bye to my friends here for some Swiss suicide party. I've got the Ukrain and that will help me get better. Come talk to Tim. He's packing a bong."

When we returned to the hollow, more people from the center had joined Tim. John Bomm and Harold Queenstreet were frail looking Americans who didn't seem to let their impending death upset their plans to party. Next to them a young Dutch guy with leukemia hunched over his crutches, and then there were two Italian women, Tia and Maria, who were never seen without the other. I had the feeling that Maria was ill and that Tia was there to support her. If I was mistaken, then I was the only healthy person around. The freak who hung out with terminally ill people to get high.

"Suck on this, Trooper, and then pass it on."

I passed the bong and melted into the endless dimensions of space while the conversation around me turned to chitchat.

"Do you have any idea how the Ostrich is going to kill himself?" Mother asked. "Poison? Hypothermia? The good old gas stove?"

"What lively conversation." The voice came from the smiling face of Arthur van Österich, who had managed to escape the siege on the lawn. He stood awkwardly in the silence his presence had on the group, as if he were waiting for an invitation and didn't feel like he could join the group freely. I understood this had to be how all celebrities felt. Normal people feel their hearts flutter a bit and get an incomprehensible thrill from proximity to fame, the moment when worries about money, relationships, and child rearing evaporate, but as soon as the stars return to the foundation of their lives, they stand alone on the outside, not knowing what to do. Van Österich probably knew that he was not in high esteem in Lowland, even though he was a patient on paper. His claims that Libertas was irresponsible in its policy on euthanasia had not gained him much popularity at the center. He was so groomed and intelligent that he seemed almost clinical, and I suddenly realized that this had probably been his lot since puberty, to be the core of every discussion, while he himself stood on the outside of life. The deep curve of his right eyebrow suggested that he had lived his days with a sneer, a substitute for some distant disappointment that suffocated and overshadowed everything he had achieved later in life.

"Go on, take a seat," Tim finally said and made room for Van Österich. Then he stood up and said: "I've got some foie gras and white wine in the fridge. I'll be back."

"Now he needs to write," Mother said. "That's Tim for you. He's always thinking and as soon as he gets an idea he's off. Don't you think his diligence is admirable, Mr. Van Österich?"

"Very," the philosopher said with a grin. "Wallace and I have had our differences, as you might know."

"Yes, and in those debates your arguments are always so childish. I don't abstain from hashish if it makes me feel slightly better. I'm told I'm getting better; in fact I'm almost fit as a fiddle. What kind of Boy Scout are you to refuse people medicine to ease their suffering, just because it makes them a bit sentimental? I would have thought that was a positive. I just can't remember seeing a child of your size before."

"Eva," I began, but that's as far as I got because she was not going to miss a second in her assault on the Ostrich.

"Have you noticed, my dear friends," she said and took a deep hit from the bong, "how brown the Ostrich's nose is on the inside?"

"Enough, Eva."

"No, it's not enough. I believe that men who have the audacity to attack my Timothy must be heartless. How dare you, if I may be so bold to ask Mr. Philosopher, belittle Tim, who is writing this remarkable story?"

That's how it had to be. Van Österich was Tim's opponent in the ideological war on death, and so he was fair game to Mother.

"People have different opinions, Mrs. Briem. I do not buy into fleeing with the aid of drugs; it's always been the basis of my theories that death calls for preparation in life. To bid adieu with dignity, people need to be in control of their lives. That's my opinion."

"And that is why you attack my dear Timothy? And maybe me, too?"

"We debate, that's all. But you should be pleased, Mrs. Briem, that your treatment is successful. The longer the drug keeps you stable, the more alternative treatments will become available to you."

Mother looked sheepishly at me and then asked the philosopher what he meant.

"There are several things in the pipelines that the doctor may not have mentioned to you. For example, the 'Master Regulator' should work on bone cancer. It may be on the common market as soon as next year. It's sort of like a vaccine that attacks the tumor directly. You could live, Mrs. Briem, even though the Ukrain fails you."

She seemed to deflate at this news. The philosopher's kindness disarmed her and made her instantly mellow. In the end she stood up and pulled him aside for a private chat behind a nearby car. They said good-bye in the driveway, Van Österich mostly intact, Mother slightly humbled.

"I asked Össi to excuse my behavior," she said as she sat down again. "It wasn't right of me to give him such a hard time."

"Össi?"

"Össi, yes. I think it suits him better," she said, explaining how it wasn't nice to speak so ill of someone who had decided to kill himself. Therefore the Ostrich would henceforth be Össi.

"Well, I did try to tell you that you were being pretty harsh."

"It's over and done with, Trooper. We separated in good spirits."

Tim returned with the foie gras and wine just as Helga was about to take the stage. She gave a moving speech, the party was set, and everyone clapped for the future of Lowland. Mother and I made a toast to her birthday and Icelandic independence, while her fellow patients cheered a triple hurrah for Iceland's Lady of the Mountain, Eva Briem Thórarinsdóttir. The doctor joined us and led the singing.

"Come with me, Willyson," he whispered and pulled me away before the cheering died out. He was in good humor and walked briskly across the lawn, claiming to have something to show me. "You won't be disappointed, I tell you. This is a glorious day, a glorious day indeed. Oh, did I mention that Helga has found an excellent Icelandic bank for our donation?"

"No!" I couldn't help myself. It was depressing to imagine the center's newfound fortune being spent on funding Danni Klambra's latest fiasco.

"You don't approve? I understand they offer the best interest rates in the country."

"Right," I said, nodding my head, unsure whether I should interfere. Inside the building the summer light crept between rooms, lighting up the colorful walls. I'd always liked the old house; there was very little reminiscent of the atmosphere I was used to finding in clinics and hospitals. The first floor was like a country home, with painted wooden furniture, bookshelves, and all sorts of upholstered sofas. This changed when we went down into the basement. We walked through a white, narrow stairwell into a fluorescent lab with steel cabinets and tables. This was where Frederik did his research, away from the outside world, growing fungi and keeping records.

"Look!" He held a test tube filled with clear liquid. "It's changed since this morning. Spore from Mr. Wallace. It's just wonderful to monitor his inner organs. I don't think I've ever had such a great opportunity to keep a record of the effects of Sativa and phenethylamines on cancer cells."

"Aren't the drugs bad for him?"

"I'm always surprised by how much the human body tolerates. Wallace has been generous with the Sativa and hasn't spared the phenethylamine. I've told him it might reduce his time on earth but he doesn't care. His main concern is getting through the day."

"So this is some sort of research into the side-effects of happiness?"

"You could say that. Wallace has given me permission to publish my findings. Timothy truly is a treasure!"

He put the test tube away and walked to a large room leading off the lab. Glass cabinets stood along the back and the shelves sprouted an assortment of old tools, instruments, and jars.

"So, here we have what I wanted you to see." He produced a little glass flask with something that looked like slimy seaweed; I thought it might be a bit of infected liver. "Your Black Beauty," he said, handing the flask to me. "It has grown and prospered like the flowers of summer. I'm sure it's the most magnificent *Afrandarius erpexoplexis* in the Northern hemisphere—it has surpassed both the *Ferflexus antarticus* and the *Norgonakis felenferosis*. I'm not sure anyone would like to have it on their face at the rate it's growing."

"I'm overcome with grief."

"You're joking, my good man, jolly good! I thought it would be nice for you to see it before you returned to the city. We humans are never alone, you know." He went on to explain how we are in fact not a single organism as most people like to think, but many, millions of coexisting organisms; the human body was more like a planet than an individual being. The heart was the sun and the brain the weather system, and the stuff in between was held together by diversity, the great cohabitation of the life units that made up every person. That's where the support from our miniscule friends, such as bacteria and fungi, really counted. "But then there are foes too, as you well know. These little terrorists are a real plague. I've seen many of them in my work, I've conquered some, surrendered to others. And so it is truly wonderful to have this new hope for Mrs. Briem."

We walked outside again, onto the lawn where Helena sat reading the same paperback she had been reading in Pleasure Fountain in the spring.

"Hi there," she said. "I was waiting for you so I could introduce your mother to Duncan. You just missed him."

"Really, Mr. Milan Kundera himself?"

"He does look a bit like him. But he's gone back to Highland for a nap. He needs a lot of sleep these days, poor Duncan."

"Eva is getting stoned anyway with Tim somewhere out there. She's in high spirits. Frederik thinks she might recover."

"That's great news."

"I'm not sure how this'll all end—the way she's going she'll end up in a reggae band with Tim before fall."

She laughed and said that this really was some trip, and how lovely it was of me to do this for my mother.

"Don't we have to try and avoid messing it up for those closest to us?"

"Perhaps. I'll get back to you on it next time."

We said good-bye and I went to fetch Mother while Ramji got ready to drive us back to the city.

"Why would you want to leave so early, Trooper? I just don't get it. Tim and I have decided to go clubbing together soon."

"Congratulations."

"You're welcome to come with us, Trooper, if you think you have the stamina and stomach for it."

"Which I'm not sure I do, Eva."

117

Chapter
12

It was just past noon when we sailed into town. Mother's veins were great rivers of happiness and it was only a matter of deciding what course they should take. Finally, she announced that the great time had come: Shopping Day. She had decided that the two of us should celebrate the miracle of Ukrain by finding a mall.

The decision didn't come as a surprise—we'd wandered into shops almost every day since we arrived in Amsterdam, buying earrings, scarves, handbags, gold-plated teaspoons with insignia, and little, carved wooden cups. I had been expecting this, but the determination in her voice and the intensity of emotion rattled me. Until now our casual shopping had been nothing more than an easy warm-up exercise, a local tournament in small sales compared to the Olympic credit card swiping we had in store. Each day had its special meaning—we'd already had Museum Day, Pub Day, Canal Day, and other similar days that differed from the days with visits to museums, pubs, and canals by being solely and solemnly devoted to museums, pubs, and canals—but Shopping Day, according to Mother's detailed journal, had not yet come to pass. It was time.

I knew how futile it was to point to all the merchandise building up in her hotel suite. Little, random bargains were ineffective in appeasing the landslide of emotions coursing through Mother's blood. If we were to have a Shopping Day we had to devote at least five hours in a mall to it, then head for Rembrandtplein to get good and drunk before taking on the charming little boutiques in the old town.

"I would expect that it's a great experience to go to a mall here. The Dutch really know their business," she said, as if the highest goal of every object was to get into a shopping bag. She had been a shopaholic ever since I could remember, especially when it came to sales. Her principles of prudence were connected to her deeply contemplative insight into Western consumerism, the river of impoverishment in which modern marketing wanted to drown people by convincing them that designer goods were superior to others. In Mother's mind, people who frequented specialty shops were devoid of any instinct of self-preservation. Or maybe it was en vogue these days to throw your wallet straight on the bonfire? Was that the smartest fuel these days? Was that what they wanted, these affected, thin men on all those ridiculous lifestyle shows?

Mother felt that one of the best virtues was to have a good eye for a bargain. She didn't mind if others, especially he-males, wanted to be a bit extravagant, pull out a Kruger '85 for instance and call for a taxi to bring them caviar. But there was a completely different approach in the domestic bookkeeping on Spítala Street. There, everything was about sorting credit card receipts from liquidations, bargain weekends at the flea market, and 2-for-1 trips to Tiger. Due to the incredible range of products available in these places, Mother could easily convince herself that she needed the most arbitrary things, like an electric can opener (Tiger: 600 krónur), a freestanding partition wall with erotic carvings (flea market: 24,000 krónur), and woolen upholstery for a car (neither place, nor price of purchase disclosed). All she needed was the car. She said I would probably thank her later: it would be nice to have extra upholstery when it got colder, it was something anyone who'd ever had a car knew, and she really thought it was quite extraordinary to have a grown man in the house and still have to go everywhere in taxcabs. I had adamantly refused to drive her around on her bargain hunts, telling her that it was the toxoplasmosis talking.

Toxoplasmosis was a disease that had frightened Mother when she first heard about it. I read her an article from a magazine shortly after I got back from Ireland. The article recounted the story of Alda Gudnadóttir, a respectable housewife who had taken diligent care of hearth and home for decades, when she suddenly became obsessed with buying consumer goods. She wanted new furniture, a new car, new clothes, even a new man, and mingled with this craving for new stuff was the pleasure she found in playing on the strings of economy. Then one day, Alda had to live with her decision of firing the help after investing in industrial cleaning products for one and a half million krónur. She had to admit to having a problem. She went to the doctor and guess what: she was suffering from toxoplasma infection!

The disease was due to a little parasite that infected the brain, causing middle-aged women to develop Crazy Cat Lady Syndrome and turn into turbulent shopaholics. Other symptoms were increased risk-taking, impulsiveness, and other effects reminiscent of having had a drink or two. Alda was treated with antibiotics and a mild sedative that brought her back to the planes of tranquility and reason. Mother, however, who, of course, suffered from this very illness as I suspected, was depressed over the news for three days until the wonderful and obvious dawned on her: She wasn't the one making unreasonable decisions. It was the parasite.

In a flash, Mother saw her financial fiascos in new light. She admitted that an overdraft of three million was quite steep, and she was grateful to me for getting her out of that pit, but when all was said and done I was in fact the one to blame for her supermarket weakness. Wasn't it I who brought Ignatius into the home all those years ago? Left him there with her when I took off and had fun with spray cans abroad? Her doctor was sure the infection came from the cat.

I plead guilty as charged, of course. The fact of the matter was that Mother was not at all displeased with her toxoplasmosis; she just wanted it to be crystal clear who was to blame when she returned from a trip into town with a seventy-thousand krónur, 100% silk pashmina. The infection was a bonus. In addition to being slightly tipsy, just at heart—was there anything as good? She'd never heard anything as absurd as getting treatment and laughed at Alda Gudnadóttir. Instead, Mother kept on purchasing: corporate staplers, necklaces, wine racks, little voodoo dolls, a tea table. To throw something away was as bad a missing out on a good bargain.

No sooner had we said good-bye to Ramji and walked into the mall, an overwhelming perfumery a few miles out of the city center, than I was saddled with a golden handbag adorned with fake pearls. Mother refused to take a bag, finding the suggestion ludicrous—putting a bag into a bag—and since she was already carrying her trusted, old purse, I was doomed to carry the new one. It didn't take long to fill it with all sorts of purchases, such as a sixteen-pound lead mobile she intended to hang from the ceiling above her bed. I tried to argue, suggesting it would upend the Feng Shui of the room. But she was no greenhorn. She knew her stuff when it came to interior design and organization. I handed over my credit card and stuffed the damn mobile into the bag.

After a rough hour of rambling aimlessly from one shop to another, I finally had the brains to withdraw 500 euros from an ATM and set Mother loose. I found an arcade, where I joined a snooker tournament with three young Vietnamese guys drinking Brazilian beer with cockroaches in the bottle. I was quite inebriated when a text came from Mother: "Am in Bar Grill Beer." I called her back but the conversation drowned in the noise of Bar Grill Beer, so I left my new friends to look for an information desk to point me in the direction of the bar. At the information desk I was told that there was no place in the complex with that name. There was, however, a place that might fit the description and sold both beer and grilled food— Crocodile Punch, which was on the first floor of the main building. When I finally found it all the effects of the Brazilian beer had worn off and a nasty hangover was starting to choke me. Mother, on the other hand, was well into her third margarita and sat smiling from ear to ear with a three-and-a-half-foot orange stuffed elephant next to her.

"What is *that*?" I asked pointing to the monstrosity.

"This? Don't you know? This just happens to be the Dutch mascot, Trooper. When I saw it I immediately thought: My super Trooper should not leave the Netherlands without one of these. And now you have one—I'm giving you this elephant."

"And what am I supposed to do with it?"

"You don't have to *do* anything with it—god, no, that's not what I mean. No, it's just for you to keep. A remembrance of our trip."

I had no qualms about getting lit out of my mind at Crocodile Punch. It was almost five when we finally got up and escaped outside to find Ramji.

"I say screw Rembrandtplein and head straight for the hotel," I said. "Hit the bong before we go out tonight."

"Trooper, darling, just because we got that stick from Tim this morning doesn't mean that today is Smoking Day. Anyway, we still have the shops downtown to visit. It's simply remarkable how quickly you become completely legless."

"I'm not legless, just a bit drrrrunk."

"Mhm. I should have known, you being a Willyson."

"I just think we should skip those stores downtown."

"No, not before I get my Buddha, it's vital that I find him today. I'm really starting to miss having my Buddha with me. That was your mistake, Hermann, leaving him behind in Iceland."

"Where would I have put it?"

"You could have made room. Just like you made room for your laptop."

"Eva, I *need* my laptop. How do you think I . . ."

"And I need my Buddha. You have your friends I have my Buddha. Ramji, Rembrandtplein, *bitte!*"

Mother's polytheism had increased in the past few years. She believed in Christ, Buddha, Muhammad Ali, Zinedine Zidane, a German gym teacher whose name she had forgotten, Berthold Brecht, and Liza Minelli. Aside from Liza, women did not easily join the ranks of the holy men, even though it was in other ways designed to honor equality and political correctness with regard to race, ethnicity, and geography. Mother loved the tangible, and so iconography seemed the most direct path to the heart of faith. She didn't seek ultimate answers, but solace, and when it came to consolation no one kicked in as well as Buddha. And she preferred a big Buddha, with a beautiful, round belly.

"Don't you think they're *too* big?" I asked when we had stopped in a little Eastern shop with icons and figurines, among which were Buddha statues that dwarfed my orange elephant.

"Oh, I'm not going to offend the great Buddha by asking if they have *smaller* ones."

I stood for a while comparing two statues. The golden one had a warm smile and radiated heroic cosmic energy, while the green Buddha had a sympathetic air that seemed to saturate the room with all-encompassing wisdom and tranquility. The former was a guide for the Red District, while the other would bring Mother numerous nights of sound sleep.

"I just don't know," I said. "It's party or peace."

"I'll take both," she replied and named the golden one Ying and the green one Yang. Ying was play and party; Yang was peace and serenity. Life was a pendulum. "What fortune, Trooper, to have such beautiful Buddhas."

The three of us took Mother by the arm and led her out of the store. I was sober again.

"Drinks on me!" she shouted and skipped into the next bar. "You have to spot me a fifty. We're doing this properly now—a pint and a chaser! Jenever is a great drink, but only if it's a double."

We sat for a couple of hours drinking. Life is a pendulum, I was either drunk or hung over, depending on whether I was inhaling or exhaling. Mother laughed at me, but took care not to overstep the line as we had yet to make it back to the hotel. Ramji had headed off to Lowland, dropping off my elephant and the other goods from the mall at our hotel. We still had the task of getting the two Buddhas back.

In the end I decided enough was enough and called a taxi. The driver was taken aback when he saw us waiting at the corner outside the bar. He added something to the meter and then we drove off with Party Buddha strapped into the passenger seat at the front, and Peace Buddha nestled between Mother and I in the back. He charged us for four passengers.

Chapter
13

And so the summer passed. June disappeared and then July, each week flying by without any disturbance in the balance of joy and sorrow. The mundane seemed to rule both my body and soul, not unlike a cold, all-consuming and immune to all cures except coffee and a pint once in a while. There was a certain calmness to everything that was very far removed from our first days in the city, a gentle rhythm that gave the waking world a routine-like hue. Every now and then a bottle of jenever would venture out of its cabinet and ask us to unite with the wonders of the world, but these moments were few and far between. Our conscious states dealt ever better with the undistorted perception of things, where everything has its place and water makes a pit stop in a glass before it travels through the body. Death was a distant neighbor who might not be meeting us down the garden path for some time. Mother left her lifesaver untouched for days on end and turned to tea drinking—green tea, rooibos tea, and chai, which she found very inspiring for yoga sessions. In this way she always had the inner strength needed for surprise outings with Timothy, who came into town every so often and took her on cannabis trips to the city's coffee shops. She made sure to tell me that even though Tim was lovely, and in some ways closer to her in character than I was, the coffee shop trips could not hold a candle to the fun we had together. She worried that I was hurt by her friendship with Tim. I took long, relieved walks and sank deep into the abyss of my own mind, my lungs steeped with more oxygen than they had enjoyed in months. On the occasions Mother appeared in my room, bored out of her mind, I would happily partake in turning life on its head at the spur of the moment, hop on a train down south to admire a royal tulip field, or order an excursion to a diamond factory. I adopted selflessness beyond all needs and inclinations.

Otherwise the days floated quietly by in Hotel Europa. I melted into the couch with my eyes on the TV remote. Although the partying was considerably subdued these days, I still suspected that my body's water percentage was no more than 40%, the rest being saturated fats and sherry. I was so bloated from drink that I could see my own face without the help of a mirror. I watched the news to convince myself that woe and misery were not mine alone. It seemed as if people were more or less hopeless: killing themselves, raping, bombing, and babbling about the ever-changing skin color of superstars in order to divert their minds from doomsday.

The TV had almost done me in one Friday morning when the phone rang, cutting through a special report on the link between cancer and artificial sweeteners. It was Helena. She said she had been thinking about what I'd said and wanted to meet up—it was important not only for Mother and Duncan, but also for everyone involved. I didn't ask her to explain, but agreed to meet her later that day by the main entrance of something she called "Artis."

"You'll find it!" she said and hung up before I had a chance to ask for directions.

★

A rtis turned out to be the name of the Amsterdam Zoo, which was just a ten-minute walk from the hotel. I arrived a good half-hour before the agreed time and I sauntered through the gates. Wherever I looked there were people strolling about in the sun, little kids with cotton candy and excited school children running around yelling at their imprisoned monkey cousins. In order to avoid the commotion, I first took a seat on a bench and then got up and walked in the opposite direction of the kids.

The zoo was built in the early nineteenth century and had a cozy old-world charm. Two golden eagles stretched out from a solid brass gate at the entrance, which was sheltered by a tunnel of trees surrounded by sculptures and glass pavilions with copper filigree. Whenever I visited such places abroad, I was reminded of the ugly streets of Reykjavík. The contrast of this garden to a street like Síðumúli, for instance, was just overwhelming. Part of the problem was the dubious city planning of talking apes like Danni Klambra, who claimed that Reykjavik's providence was embedded in the plastic houses he and his father had planned for the city center. Although there was no arguing that the Klambra boys were the human equivalent to a scrap heap, their aesthetic sensibilities were not unique. It was a global trade. Even here in Amsterdam you could find buildings that were acts of terror toward people with human emotions.

I stood in front of a menagerie of endangered European mammals wishing there was similar cage for Danni Klambra, wondering if the problem could be traced to the same degenerate hole spawning the news on TV. Two World Wars, nuclear bombs, and genocide had not sufficed to cull our numbers; we reproduced like termites and eliminated other species that stood in our way. Was there any hope? For me? For Mother? I was submerged in these pessimistic thoughts when I caught a glimpse of my watch and realized

Helena could appear any minute. I walked back to the entrance and found her at the ticket booth.

"Hi." She took me by the hand and led me to a restaurant within the zoo. "I've been thinking about what you said and I think you're right: you'll never be able to forgive yourself if you mess it up for those closest to you."

We waited while a waiter in a green uniform took our order and brought us a couple of Cokes; then she continued.

"The thing is that I've always done everything my way. When I was fifteen I took off from Highland and moved into a closet with two gays on Koestraat. I felt the rest of the world could just fuck off. I had lost my mother and ended up with Duncan against my will. He took me in because no one else knew what to do with me, and I don't know if I've ever forgiven him for his kindness. It wasn't Duncan's fault that I lost my mom, but I blamed him because he took her place. And what happens is that you get stuck in some hole that you can't get back out of. I was just a kid, of course, but I often think that I was quite selfish. There must have been others who were sad as well."

She seemed to be slowly honing in on the purpose of this meeting. I still didn't quite grasp how she and Duncan were connected, but I sensed that I was a participant in the solution of this philosophical issue of having a parent.

"Maybe it's just selfish wanting to fix things if the only goal is to be able to forgive yourself," she went on. "But still. Isn't all sense of morality selfish by that definition? I suppose it's childish to think like this. I come to some conclusion confirming how mature I am, but then it makes no sense to me after a few months. I want to know. Do I think that I'm wise because I've really grown up or because I'm young and stupid? To be young—is that to want to change the world? Or is it all a cliché? I suppose there's no way of knowing what the future version of yourself will be."

I would have liked to agree, claim life didn't map out the future in any way but kept you in constant *excitement*, that we floated in a happy vacuum toward the next unexpected miracle. A long time ago I had thought these same thoughts, felt the mutations in my soul, experienced diversity in the constant progression of the days, and thought that the concept of maturity was synonymous with wisdom and inner peace, long before the love in my heart outweighed the sorrow it had become.

"If you really were young and stupid you'd never imagine you were young and stupid," I said.

"But that doesn't mean that I'm an adult. I'm simply starting to doubt all of this."

"To simply doubt everything is to be an adult."

"I don't think you're as messed up as you claim to be. If you were that stagnant, you'd never have come on this trip."

"Well. I do have the body of a sixty-year-old woman, according to my doctor."

She finished her Coke and returned to the subject, talking about Duncan's illness, which was the reason she called me in the first place. He had one of those types of cancer people somehow learn to live with, never quite at death's door but still only half there. Now he hung out at home in Highland using his illness as an excuse for doing nothing, which was very unlike the old Duncan, who felt that everything but dancing on tables was a waste of time.

"So I was thinking—if your mom's lonely and Duncan's lonely, maybe we should arrange for them to meet."

I was beginning to see the light. Milan Kundera and the Knight in the Kilt embodied in a dying lord in the countryside . . .

"I know it's a bit far-fetched," she said, cutting off the violins that had started playing in my head, "but it wouldn't hurt having a little party. It was Gloria's idea. She thinks the two of them might hit it off."

"So this is the professional opinion of a matchmaker?"

"Exactly. This is a professional opinion."

We stood up and sealed the deal with a handshake before strolling back to the gate. We would meet in Lowland at the end of August after Helena came back from her trip and when the guesthouse restaurant would be available for a garden party, some nice afternoon when the hottest summer days were over.

I was happy to have a few weeks to prepare for the party. Ambiguous activity scratched at my core and wouldn't let me be no matter how I tried to ignore it. Black, white, black, white, black: this sudden dazzling light in the eyes of my emotional life had steadily amplified over the past weeks. I was gripped by extreme optimism that immediately vaporized into the grayness of rainclouds until it opened up again and retreated, hovering for a moment until I came to myself and everything went still, just a slight breeze under the cloud bank; I sat down and surrendered to the gloom.

When I returned to the hotel there was a party in the lobby. My good friend Dmitri wanted me to drink a Guinness with champagne to show foreign guests how people had survived in Iceland since the ninth century, but I wasn't in the mood.

Instead I made some chai and exposed myself to the bathroom mirror. I just had to lean a little to the right for my body to be entirely on one side. My torso actually resembled another face: the eyebrows of the red nipple-eyes had not been groomed for a very long time, the round bellybutton-mouth was slightly droopy and adorned with a moustache, surprised by an ever-expanding chin that seemed to stretch further out into the world, munching on the only organ of mine that had the slightest potential of having an impact on the future.

I had known for a while that I needed a change of lifestyle, though not by depriving Mother of her parties or giving up on our adventure—we had come too far for that. The proof was in my morning breath, this green odor that answered if I huffed into my palm and sniffed. It was in my shapeless muscles, deteriorating posture, fatigue, memory loss, and the unpleasant fact that my face was completely androgynous after a close shave. Mother was becoming less and less dependent on her lifesaver and stuck mostly to her chai, which released her from the pressures of drinking wine; the opportunity to not consume 3,000 extra calories a day in the form of alcohol was simply too good to miss. For the first time ever, I decided with rock-solid determination to lose weight. I would cry over my fate until the corpse rose out of the haze; life would fill my body and I would become aware each waking hour that I was among the living. Without gulping down sherry-cola, without wanting to throw up after heartfelt canoodling with a leg of ham.

The effort started as expected with hunger pains and torment in the hotel gym. For the first three days I was convinced I was about to die. When I woke up on the fourth morning I was sure I had moved up a level of existence, had obtained new karma after a sad demise on a squat machine in Hotel Europa. But due to the mercilessness of the higher powers I had woken up in my room as if nothing had happened. Mother didn't know how to take these antics of mine. On one hand, nothing was quite as pathetic as a man on a diet, but on the other hand there was the upside, the possibility that I might snag a girlfriend. Over time she'd gotten used to me going on the occasional fat-burning stint, eating vegetables to wean my stomach off fatty foods and ordering white wine in restaurants instead of my beloved lager. Mother would use the opportunity to ask for a pint and a schnapps, laughing hysterically when the waiters got it wrong and switched the drinks in front of us. It was always funny when I was the girl. It did me no good to point indignantly to her potbelly. Unlike me, she was simply a woman who filled out her dresses, her feminine curves healthy for her age; quite a few people would call them erotic. "You, Trooper, however, are fat."

But when she took a peek into the hotel gym and saw I was serious, she seemed to have a change of heart. Maybe all this running would bring out the long-awaited correction to my physique that was owed to us by the creator? She had always been astounded by how unfortunately one genetic pool could line up. Despite sincere efforts of the parents to create a healthy child, everything had gone topsy-turvy in this conception. The slightness that characterized Willy's bulk had been passed on to me, but lengthwise; I grew outward, so my size was all horizontal. In fact, everything about me but my build should have made me petite.

"But now you'll fix that, Trooper," she said as she got ready to leave the gym. "I think it's heroic of you to do this now, while you're still almost young. Some people never get rid of the blubber. Just carry all that weight through marriages and divorces, all the way to the grave. Like old Edda. We had to have a custom-made coffin for her."

She said good-bye and left me to struggle with the bench press. In the roughly three weeks leading up to the party I lost 16 and a half pounds so fast that I looked slightly hollow. The bathroom mirror could hardly keep up with my dwindling body. My facial expressions became more apparent, my nose declared independence from my cheeks, and my body took on human form.

My diet was not without sacrifice. One day, as I was jogging down the hotel stairs with *All Time Power Ballads* channeling from my iPod into my ears, I had, without noticing (at first very quietly, or so I was told, but then steadily increasing in volume until it resonated throughout the entire gym), started singing along, soaring up to the high notes with Nilsson as he sang beautifully:

> *I can't li-iii-iii-ve*
> *If living is without you . . .*

It wasn't until the gym's supervisor snatched the headphones from my ears that I heard how clear and sincere my singing was.

Chapter
14

On a bright Saturday toward the end of August, Ramji picked us up at Hotel Europa to drive us to the party. The Ambassador snaked through the streets and we left the city at the pace of the settling dusk, under a half-clouded rural sky that floated huge shadows across the land.

"This is wonderful!" Mother said. "What a country we're in, Trooper. The town we just passed was almost like Koeningsdorf in Germany."

"I know, it's great."

"Is India this lovely, Ramji, or maybe even more beautiful?"

"Very beautiful, Mam," Ramji replied absentmindedly. He had been unusually shifty and had hardly uttered a word as we passed through one village after the other.

"Is everything ok, Ramjiminn?"

"Yes. Ok, Mam BriemMam. Except . . . no, it's nothing."

Mother and I exchanged surprised looks.

"You don't have to be shy about it, Ramji, if there is something bothering you, my dear," she said and adopted a very saintly expression. "But you know this, of course, coming from the birthplace of Buddha himself. One needs to flow with the life force. Not allow the troubles of our everyday life to create obstacles."

"Yes, Mam."

"Philosophy aside, Ramji," I inserted. "Is there something bothering you?"

"Yes, maybe a bit. I was thinking, Mr. Trooper, whether you remember Mr. Bubi, sir? Bubi Rotandari?"

"The taxi guy? Is he on your case again?"

"Don't be so negative, Trooper," Mother said. "Perhaps there is good news."

"Right. Ramji?"

"He said, sir . . . He said that he wanted to meet Mr. Hermann and speak to him. He said that it's important, sir. Business. I think he means you, sir."

"Of course he means me. He's insane."

"Yes, sir."

"Isn't it enough that he pinned me to the a sidewalk?" I asked, but Ramji was not to keen to recall the conflict in Nieuwenmarkt.

"Mr. Bubi says that Mr. Hermann, that is you, Mr. Trooper, he says that you can find him a place to keep the cars."

"What?"

"Yes, Mr. Trooper, that is what he said. That you can find a place to keep the cars."

I told Ramji to tell Mr. Bubi that I had nothing to say to him. The panic in the driver's eyes intensified.

"Did he threaten to do something to you, Ramji, if you didn't get me to talk to him?"

"Mr. Bubi does not make threats, Mr. Trooper, but I know him. He is not like other men. He is very determined."

"Determined, hah! This guy, a crazy Indian who beat the shit out of me for being a racist, now wants me to find him a garage."

"Are you a racist now?" Mother asked.

"No, I . . . oh, forget it."

"Do you know anything about this, Ramji?" Mother asked again and leaned over the front seat. "Trooper is upset because I don't ask the right questions. But do you know anything? Who is this man he's talking about?"

"Mr. Bubi, Mam, my old boss. He owns the largest taxi company in Amsterdam."

"Oh, you hear that, Trooper? Your new friend is a great man."

I told her that this man, who attacked me at the racist ball and then wiped the sidewalk with my face, was not at all great, but she felt I was being petty.

"Weren't you just being offensive? Without noticing? Isn't that what you're always saying to me? That I'm a racist and god knows what without realizing it? Well, who's to say that you're not guilty of the very same thing yourself?"

I didn't bother answering her. Mother had clearly decided whose side she was on and was just getting started.

"If there is some wrong there," she continued, "something you've done to him, you'll get it fixed, Trooper. The largest taxi company! I think this is something for you to consider, with all those bills at the hotel."

She took a little sip of her lifesaver to mark the end of her speech and then continued talking to Ramji. We drew closer to Lowland. As we passed a motorcycle parked at the side of the driveway with "Rent your own taxi from Rotandari Taxi" plastered on the side, Mother expressed her delight. "Look at that, Trooper. It's a self-taxi. I don't think I've seen anything as brilliant."

Mr. Bubi Rotandari stood in the middle of the courtyard, a sapphire blue turban on his head and the soft breeze in his impressive beard.

"Mr. Hermann!" he shouted when we got out of the car. "You've come to do business. Good." He smiled, walked over and embraced me, lifting me a good five inches off the ground before introducing himself to Mother. "I am Bubi Rotandari. Hermann and I are great friends. He is going to help me find a place in Iceland for my taxis."

"In Iceland?" I was taken aback. "What are you going to do there?"

"We'll see, Mr. Hermann. First we should go to the back where people are waiting. When everyone has a full belly we can talk business. Never talk business when hungry."

He led us across the parking lot in front of the guesthouse and into an enclosed garden behind the restaurant, where Gloria and Steven seemed to be having trouble with a gas heater. I almost didn't recognize the doctor's son; he'd put on so much weight over the summer. Helena sat in the middle of the garden, basking in the sun with Dr. Frederik and a stout man who had to be Duncan: a cheerful type with a friendly aura, gray hair, and a dark tan. He was dressed in a white short-sleeved shirt and a blue and green tartan kilt.

"MacKenzie tartan," he said when we walked over to the round table and he caught Mother staring. "I like to dress up for special occasions. If there's anything I miss from the old Highlands it's being allowed to dress like a lady." He stood up and kissed Mother's hand. "Duncan MacKenzie, pleased to meet you."

"Eva Briem," Mother replied. "And if I may say so—you don't look the slightest bit ladylike."

"I should hope not," Duncan laughed. "There's nothing quite as comfortable as a kilt." His grin highlighted his handsome face. A bit more heavyset than Milan Kundera, he was a he-male nonetheless. "Now, I have to ask you to excuse me while I go and get Monica to bring us more ale."

"Who is this Monica person?" Mother asked, leaning up against me when the lord was gone.

"Monica runs the restaurant," Helena explained. "It's not a very rewarding job, I think. It's never really busy."

"I try to look in on Monica as often as I can," the doctor said and greeted us with a handshake. "It's good to have a little walk and refreshment once in a while."

Helena insisted that the place would have gone under without him and Duncan. The doctor agreed, explaining that he was now legally a Dutchman. "And Duncan's a Scot. Both great beer nations."

"At least while you hang in there," Helena said.

"Have you met everyone, Mr. Hermann?" Bubi asked, pointing to each and everyone present. "The woman in the corner is Gloria. She is a matchmaker. Next to her is a puffy man with a gas heater." Bubi described everything to me as if I were blind. "That man is Steven. I will not tell you his business because Nanak Dev does not approve. But are they not your friends, Mr. Hermann? It should be you introducing us."

Bubi Rotandari roared with laughter at his lame joke. I downed my beer in one gulp to calm my nerves, relieved by the immediate effects of the alcohol. Mother felt I was being vulgar and asked them to excuse my behavior; I was just like my father, getting drunk off a thimbleful of wine. We were headed for an interesting evening.

"She's a piece of work, my Monica," Duncan said as he returned, splashing beer out of the jugs he was carrying. "She refuses to speak to me."

"Do you think that might have something to do with you leaving her at the altar?" Helena asked.

"It's not that I don't like her," Duncan replied. "Monica's a wonderful cook. But as I stood there in that church, it just dawned on me that it's not healthy for a man of my size to marry for food."

"Very wise," Mother said. "One should always marry for love."

I was expecting a speech on Willy Nellyson to follow that statement, but fortunately Duncan took the floor, bellowing a few words on love and friendship in his thick Scottish accent. It sounded as if his mouth were full of mashed potatoes. Gloria and the doctor's son joined us. He brought the gas heater and complained about the cold, saying he'd read that half the globe would soon be covered in ice.

"Then I will open IceTaxi in India," Bubi said.

"Even scientific invention has its downside," the doctor replied. "We tame the natural forces and cultivate this land of ours that is below sea level, but where will it end? I'm afraid it will all go under water."

"Listen to you lot!" Helena said, pointing to the men. "You're chauffeured everywhere you go, burping beer, while my generation gets to deal with the shit."

"Your generation is infertile," Bubi Rotandari said. "Here, those men who are not homos have useless genitals. The Netherlands have the smallest population growth since the war."

"Are there no homosexuals in India?" Mother asked.

"Only in Mumbai. But we have too many people there, anyway."

140

"I worried for a while that my Trooper would turn out that way," Mother said, patting the back of my hand. "But my Trooper is safe now, aren't you? You wouldn't start letting someone tap your keg at this age, right?"

"It should not be allowed," Bubi Rotandari said, taking a swig of his beer. "It is against God and the nation."

"God is a fickle fellow," Duncan said with a vague smile, hoping to loosen things up a bit. "I'm sure, though, that he would agree with us asking Monica to top us up again."

"You go, Trooper," Mother said and placed her hand lightly on the lord's shoulder to stop him. "It's not right to have Duncan running back and forth all the time."

She smiled and crossed her leg over the other so it pointed toward him. Compared to the long-range weapons I pretended to possess in my arsenal for communicating with women, her military strategies were blitzkrieg. Duncan flattered Mother and she accepted his compliments with the ease of someone who has mastered the warfare of love. The tarot cards didn't lie. The knight in the kilt leaned over and whispered something in her ear.

"I need a doctor," Mother said, laughing at his joke. "Your tricks will kill me!"

In that instance Monica walked in to announce that dinner was ready and that she needed a few good men to carry the feast out. Helena and Ramji stood up to make room for the cook. She took two bowls of pheasant crackling from a basket and placed them on the table.

"A gift from Nanak Dev," Bubi said, munching on the rind. "Most excellent, Mrs. Monica, you are a servant of life to bring us such a delicacy." The cook nodded, stood up, and disappeared back inside the building. "Rotandari men eat game, no problem. Bird meat. Animal meat. Horse meat. We are Sikhs."

"Like my Ramji," Mother said.

"I am a Catholic, Mam," Ramji said. He and Helena seemed to be carrying all the food reserves of the world on one enormous plate. The feast was the same Mother and I had enjoyed on our special Friday in Amsterdam, when everything was new and the quest for special drinks stretched into the night. The centerpiece was a whole roasted pig, stuffed with pheasant and bacon rinds, with vegetables packed all around it.

"Incredible food!" Mother said and competed for the crackle with Steven, who loved calories with the same passion he had for diminishing their effects on other people. He ate one quail after the other with cream, bacon, and several pints of Shakespeare ale. He seemed to have lost the aversion he had to food the first time we met.

"BodySnatch," Gloria explained. "He's fulfilling his dream."

When everyone had eaten, Bubi Rotandari turned to the real reason for showing up at the party. It turned out that his great uncle, Binu Fagandi, had recently been in Iceland to cash in bank shares his daughter had won in a poker game. During his stay in that dark and harsh country, Binu Fagandi had noticed several things: for instance, that one taxi from the airport to the city cost the same as running the school bus in Haridwar, his hometown, for three whole months. Short of cash, Fagandi had been stuck for two days in a rather grubby hostel near the bus station before finally managing to cash in the shares. The light-hearted relief sparked an idea in Mr. Fagandi's mind: Iceland needed a taxi company run by the Rotandaris.

"And there you have it. You need cheap taxis in Iceland and so Mr. Hermann is going to help me."

"I absolutely agree," Mother said. "I live on Spítala Street, which is downtown, and it costs me more than 10 euros to take a taxi home."

"You are right, Mam," Bubi replied. "My uncle Binu says that in Iceland there are too many cars that nobody wants. Icelanders are very stupid. They keep their cars on ugly tarmac and take expensive taxis."

"You seem to know everything about Iceland, Herr Bubi."

"Yes. I bought ten cars from Mr. Sigmund, who is from Zwickau and lives in Iceland. He sold me Honda Civic and Citroën, but also a Trabant with an electrical motor. Those cars only use two liters of diesel for one hundred kilometers. Now I have ten taxis in Iceland. *Krónubílar.* They are my pride and joy. The Crown Cars. IceTaxi."

"Marvelous! Trooper!" Mother exclaimed. "Now you can really use taxis."

Bubi seized the opportunity to point out that I would have to assist him and ignored my protests by holding up a hand in front of my face: an impenetrable wall indicating his authority. "Mr. Hermann, you'll do this to fulfill your duty to me. You will not regret it."

"You'll never get the permits you need," I said, but Bubi waved a document contradicting my case.

"You will find me a place, Mr. Soldier, because you know people."

He had hardly finished the sentence when a brilliant light clicked on in my mind. I stood up from the table and walked into the guesthouse where Monica kept a small computer. My plan was even more ingenious than any manipulated love affair of the elderly. It was the greatest scheme in human history. After ten minutes of surfing the web I pulled Danni Klambra's business card out of my pocket and made a phone call. I explained in detail what I wanted. This would have to go off without a hitch.

"No problem, my man," Daniel said, clueless to the Hell on Earth awaiting him. "We'll take care of it. Get your guy to check in on us in Herengrach and we'll call it even. And then we're squared, H. Done. D.O.N.E. Okay?"

I hung up and walked out to Bubi and Ramji waiting by the Ambassador.

"It's done," I said. "Your Uncle Binu will get the building he needs in Iceland, Mr. Bubi, but you must listen very carefully: This list has all the buildings on the market, and it also states the price."

I handed him a printout of the real estate listings I'd found on the Internet. He looked carefully at the photos and peered at me.

"You just need to know one thing, Mr. Bubi, and that is that these guys are supposed to give you a good discount. You make sure you get a really good deal, whatever the building. He will try to worm his way out of it, but then you say to him: 'I am Bubi Singh Rotandari from India. I will not budge.' You tell him you are my friend and if he doesn't come through for you he will be betraying our friendship and all Rotandaris who have ever been, and you tell him that if he betrays you, you know where he lives and with whom he does business, and what kind of business that is. You tell him what fate awaits those who cross Rotandaris. If you do this, your Uncle Binu will get the building he wants at the price he wants. And now I believe our business is concluded."

Bubi Rotandari said nothing. He smiled because I had understood him. Our two worlds had collided for a moment and we had seen eye to eye. Bubi got on his bike, tore up the pebbled courtyard with his back wheel in a pale dust cloud, and blasted down the driveway, disappearing out onto the main road.

"Now Bubi is gone, Mr. Trooper, sir," Ramji said.

"Good riddance."

"Mr. Bubi is Sikh, sir. He came to this country with his father, Bir Singh Rotandari, when he was fifteen years old. They left India because it was not a good place for the Sikhs at that time."

"I've heard about that. Indira Gandhi, right? They killed her?"

"Ah, you know, Mr. Trooper?" Ramji was surprised but continued: "It is true, she was killed, but it was not that simple. Our Prime Minister, Mam Gandhi, was extremely popular. The people loved her because she was just and cared for the people and the future. She cared for the Hindus and the Christians and the Muslims and the Sikhs and the Buddhists; all Indians had the same Prime Minister. I know, Mr. Trooper, that when you say 'they killed her' you are thinking of the Sikhs. And it was true, it was a Sikh who murdered Indira, but one Sikh is not all Sikhs so it is not right to think badly of them all. I am a Christian and want to forgive like Christ teaches. The same for Hindus, they must forgive. But people don't always do as they believe. They threw stones at Sikhs and chased them. They burned their stores and wrecked their cars, and chased them out of their homes. Many left the country and went to the West, like Bubi and his father. When I came to the Netherlands, Mr. Bubi took me and put me behind the wheel of one of his taxis and gave me a salary, food, and a home. I had to work hard but he was fair and I worked for him for two years. I sent the money to Nainital, my village in India. But when I met Dr. Frederik and he wanted me to drive for him, Mr. Bubi wanted money. I am not a slave, Mr. Trooper. He should not have done this, but he did it anyway. Dr. Frederik paid a lot of money so I could come and work for him. A lot of money—that Mr. Bubi got for nothing. He was not the owner of me, but that is how it happened."

"I'm sorry, Ramji, the world is full of people like that."

"I know, sir."

"People do what they will. They go as far as they can to get what they think is theirs by right."

"Not everyone, Mr. Trooper. Not everyone. There is still hope in the world."

"You think so?"

"I know so," he said and walked back with me to the party.

Chapter
15

The gathering had grown when Ramji and I returned. A ten-gallon belly with a woman attached sat surrounded by a rugby huddle of small children and a bearded man waving tubs of ice cream at them to try and charm them off her. Mother watched the family wearily and was obviously rather fed up. She lit up a cigarette and retreated into another dimension. I walked over to Helena, who stood in the doorway wrestling with a beer keg. She told me that she doubted that the tap had seen as much use in a single day since the pub opened in the eighteenth century. "But it seems to do the trick, look at them."

"Yup. Skirts will fly back at Duncan's tonight, Scottish and Icelandic."

"No matter what happens later when everyone has sobered up. You should fetch the glasses. I think I've got this fixed."

I was happy when I walked back out into the garden, dying with anticipation to get back to the tap.

"The truth of detox is found in the joy of the retox, Trooper," Mother said and handed me the tumblers. "I could see it in you, after you started spending all that time in the gym. Old Edda always used to say the same thing. The whole point of a healthy lifestyle is to have the capacity to go overboard. Did you know that Gloria is a matchmaker?" She pointed over to her and the doctor's son. "That explains how she found such a good man."

"Actually, Steven and I wouldn't have met if it weren't for Trooper," Gloria said. "I would say, judging from experience, that Icelanders are good matchmakers."

"Ah, but bad at matching up," Mother insisted. "Everyone in Iceland is unhappy. That's a fact."

"That's not entirely true, Eva," I objected. "Life isn't so simple. We look for love, find it, and then lose it, just like everybody else."

"You're quite the poet today, Hermann."

"I'm not drinking fast enough. This is a hangover."

"If only you were like this every time you got hung over, Trooper. Then Iceland would have a great poet. But please get a refill, it should last until tomorrow."

When Helena and I returned, Gloria and Steven had sneaked off for a smoke and the old folks sat debating the Hippocratic Oath. The doctor said it was questionable in modern context.

"I've always maintained that in order to be a good doctor one has to take the Hippocratic Oath with a pinch of salt," he said. "To me, the patient and his wishes are the ultimate factor."

"I suppose suicide is the only thing in life that you can never regret?"

"You're funny, Mrs. Briem," the doctor laughed. "Can I use this on the cynics when I go to my convention in December?"

"Of course. But now I want to propose a toast to Helena because she is as beautiful as I was when I was young. And to Trooper, the reason I got to know all you wonderful people."

"To Trooper!"

The commotion seemed to invigorate the rugby huddle's ADHD, one kid after the other pulling its head out of the ice cream and zipping around the garden.

"I wish she'd leave and take her brood with her," Mother said, her patience wearing thin. "I can't understand why people don't leave their kids at home when they go to restaurants. Fidgety little kids don't mix well with drinks."

"Little darlings," the doctor said. "I've always liked having children pattering about."

"That's because you are a child in retirement," Duncan said. "I've never known a grown man who could become as absorbed in his interests as you."

"I think someone should go and have a word with her." Mother continued to criticize the pregnant woman, who she felt must have been mentally challenged from birth, thick as a brick, and this herd of hers was yet more proof of the decline of civilization. Good people were brainwashed in educational institutions that made them depressed so they delayed having offspring until they were well past their prime, while idiots bred like rabbits, making the intelligent people more miserable and inevitably single. "Trooper has a kid in Africa," she suddenly said. "Kakebe, a nice boy in Kenya."

"Kakebe is actually Zola's kid now," I said, not liking where this was going. Mother hardly ever mentioned Kakebe unless she was planning an invasion into the past. "I think she was going to visit him."

"You weren't supportive enough," she said and complained about my part in human suffering. "You can say what you like about Zola, but you were not there for her when it came to this."

"What was I supposed to do? Fly to Africa on the weekends with a football to play with him? He was just a little kid in Kenya who didn't know us at all."

"Really? Well, maybe you'll think about what has become of the youth in this world when you get to my age. Especially if she keeps on going, that ever-breeding, conservative ogre. How come it's only the idiots that have children these days? Do you know, Duncan?"

"It's a travesty. One hundred thousand people are born in the Netherlands each year and they're all imbeciles."

"That's why I'm always going on about this to Trooper. I tell him it's fun to have kids."

"Families are not just based on fun and games," I said.

"Well they're hardly built on people keeping to themselves into old age, either," she shot back. "How old are you now, Trooper? Getting ever closer to my age, I warn you. And Helena is twenty-three. That was considered quite old to be childless in my day. Maybe you'll have lots of kids when you get to the fashionable age, which seems to be around forty these days, then you can have a hip replacement done at the same time. You'll be fitted with a pace-maker to make it through the kids' teens. My opinion is that it's best to get it done sooner, than later. You don't have to get married and live happily ever after."

"Give it a rest, Eva," I said as Helena headed over to the beer tap with a funny smile on her face.

"You just be yourself and I'm sure she'll consider it," Mother continued. "Now that you don't have that mole in your face. What do you think, Duncan, don't you think Helena and Trooper would have a nice looking child?"

"I'm sure of it," Duncan laughed. "But I don't think we'll have any say in the matter. My Helena goes her own way and I'm sure that Trooper does too."

Mother stared downcast into the void, let down by Duncan's lack of enthusiasm for getting Helena and me into one bed. I felt the need to calm her down and used the opportunity while Helena was away to promise that if we both ended up single and had no other chance of procreating, if Helena's womb was about to cave in, and my sperm count was seriously dwindling on account of too much microwaved food, I would ask her to do this for the love of humanity. I would make a hospital appointment, even if I had to take ten Viagra and read a dozen porn magazines with young middle-aged women, I would do it—squeeze out the last drops into a cup, my semen brown from age but still vibrant, full of little swimmers screaming to become bigger and to get to rule the world, lick lollipops and eat chocolate cake, rent slasher movies. We would not become extinct: our love of alcohol, fatty foods, and fun would live on, all the charming needs and vices, all the crazy nights and the wonder-genes that got people dancing on tables in their old age, that is how our offspring would wind up, a gray-haired child with rosy cheeks after a series of special drinks.

"Slow down, Hermann," Mother said and told me that the night was young and there was plenty of time left for spewing out drunken philosophy. "I think little Eva will make her own decisions. A grandchild, how great! Did you hear that, Duncan? A little baby!"

I'd had enough of this pseudo-child and pointed out that the world's variables were numerous: I could move to Thailand, open up a pizza parlor by a swimming pool; and Helena might become the Secretary General of the Council of Europe. If so, there was hardly much sense in making a baby who would be flung around the world in airplanes for the sole reason of providing us with physical proof of our existence. And what if the plane crashed? Wouldn't we all die anyway? What was the point of life when all was said and done?

"For the love of God, Trooper."

"More beer," Duncan said when Helena returned and filled our glasses. "I suppose the point of life might as well be to drink a bit of Shakespeare ale. At least today. *Grüss Gott!*"

"*Grüss Gott.*" Mother raised her glass. "Now we just need a little schnapps to make it perfect."

*

We were all pretty drunk when Helga turned up to the party. She smiled wistfully and asked the doctor to have a word. Then she gave us a little wave and left.

"I suspected as much," the doctor said. "Timothy Wallace has completed his book. Helga stood the last watch by him."

*

Sorrow manifests in various ways. Some people order a Hummer with strippers, like the Klambra boys did when the don passed, but at the round table in the garden people seemed to be on the same page. We stood up, held hands, and paid our respects to the deceased. Then we started to clear the table and carry the glasses and plates inside. Mother said that if Timothy wasn't a miracle worker by finishing his autobiography so soon, and in his state of health, there were no miracle workers in this world. When I told her the truth, that Tim's last breath was in the final page of the script, she laughed in surprise. It had to be a joke. Timothy couldn't be dead. Was I joking? "Trooper, are you joking?"

She was inconsolable for a while and I handed her tissues, my shoulder, anything she could cry into, until I led her to the Ambassador where Ramji stood waiting with the doctor and Duncan. We decided that the chauffeur would drive the old folks back to Highland. Mother could have a nap while the rest of us could have an early wake for Timothy in the Scotsman's home. We would stay the night so Ramji wouldn't have to drive us into the city.

"It's always sad when people die," Gloria said as we watched the car disappear. "I only met Tim once but I know he wanted it this way. This is how life goes around here, people come to this place to die. I've learned from my father-in-law not to be upset when people get what they want."

"But did you see Eva's reaction?"

"Well, your Mother is sad because her friend died."

"And how do you think she'll react if she has to go the same way? The doctor might be optimistic, but you never know. I dread the day when she has to make this choice."

We stood up from the bench and met Helena, who was going to clear out Tim's room and then catch a lift with Helga into town. Steven and Gloria decided to walk with me to Highland. I was once again gripped by that strange numbness that had haunted me now and then these past weeks in Amsterdam: blinding optimism that illuminated the moment and froze it before it disappeared.

"I feel sick." Steven had turned deadly pale and stopped in the middle of the road. "I think I need to throw up."

"If you can just keep it down . . ." Gloria began but didn't finish the sentence because Steven ran to the side of the road, leaned forward, and puked.

"I'll call Ramji and ask him to bring the doctor," I said.

"I don't want dad," Steven whimpered between hurls. "I'm trying to expand my stomach. Sometimes I eat too much."

"I'll wait until he feels better. You go on, Trooper, it's just a short walk. See you soon."

When I came to the house Mother was already asleep in one of the guestrooms, but Duncan and the doctor sat chatting in the lounge. The Scotsman was preparing drinks.

"We were just talking about when Helena first came to live here all those years ago," the doctor said, handing over his empty glass. "I don't think any man has been as strangely entangled into a single line of females as you have, Duncan. It's quite an endeavor."

"And that's why I don't do it to myself or others to broach that topic."

"Well," said the doctor, "I must say that I think that your amorous adventures should be part of the curriculum in every school. Such astonishing fiascos should be a lesson to all men."

"What happened?" I asked. I had been intrigued by the relationships in Highland for a long time. "Helena told me you're not her grandfather."

"Not exactly, but almost. I'm kind of her grandfather, kind of her dad. No wonder the poor lass has chosen the road less travelled. Even though my Helena is the only thing I can truly be proud of, I have to admit that the story behind our relationship is not to my credit."

"That's true," the doctor agreed. "Sadly enough."

"Has she told you something about those early days?" the Scotsman asked. "People running wild around here, naked and sky high, in some sort of community I chose to call a commune. This went on into the eighties, long after most such enterprises had fallen flat.

People's hair stood on end, straight out from the body, because that's what the so-called sexual revolution meant, people were cold. But then one day love came a-knocking, in a smile belonging to a woman called Hanna. I was instantly convinced that my idiocy was a thing of the past. The commune was disbanded and we shacked up. Six months later she was diagnosed with breast cancer and she was gone within the year. I was crushed, didn't care about anything. I disgraced all forms of life with my apathy toward it. Of course I should never have come near my stepdaughter, but I did."

"Oof," Frederik said.

"Aye," Duncan agreed. "A week after Hanna died, her daughter Gabriela showed up for the funeral. She had been living with her dad in England and we'd never met before. I was in shock. There out in the courtyard stood the spitting image of my Hanna, just twenty years younger. Disaster ensued."

"He got into her panties," Frederik said, cutting to the chase.

"Gabriela and I hit it off, her presence brought me some consolation. Before I knew it she was in my arms, I gave her a peck on the cheek, tasted her tears. I was so full of self-pity and delusions that I let myself believe that I was happy. This went on for a couple months, but then I sent her back to England. It's human to err, but to continue that messed up relationship was utterly insane. And it's no excuse, though my good friend Fred kept telling me so, that I was not myself after Hanna died."

"And so I stopped," Frederik said. "It's becoming more and more clear as time goes by that this was quite the mess you created. Well, it would be, if not for Helena."

"Yes. In the end Gabriela shared her mother's fate. The cancer had taken its toll when she reappeared on my doorstep with little Helena in tow, twelve years after I sent her packing. They stayed with me for the two months it took Gabriela to die. Helena remained. She's my daughter, even though she always just calls me Duncan."

"And that's enough for now," the doctor said. "I think that's Steven walking up the path, and correct me if I'm wrong, Trooper, but isn't that your mother standing there in the doorway? Before I head back to Lowland I would like to raise my glass to Eva Briem who is awake, and to Timothy Wallace from Missouri who doesn't have to suffer another second. Rest in peace, my friend. *Grüss gott.*"

Chapter
16

O ver the next few days, after the party, the city seemed to show a different face; it seemed botoxed and softer, but also without any expression. The evenings were a still life of a recently passed time, a paused promotional video, a piano sonata to highlight an image of a sunrise-red canal at the end of the day's broadcast. The world was in slow motion, waiting to become new, as if this version had been played too many times over.

Initially we'd only planned to stay a few weeks in this place. I'd always meant to find us an apartment, a more affordable hotel, or even a boat on one of the canals, but I'd let it slide for longer than my bank account could allow, drenched in weirdness and a gift for procrastination and postponement that echoed through the escapades of my hangover. Our spending at Hotel Europa was starting to create pressure on the exchange rate of the Icelandic Króna, which was plummeting daily. There was something going on up in Iceland that I didn't grasp and didn't care to explore, but it was starting to hurt. The bare necessities, such as soap and ham, suddenly started to feel like risk capital investments. I haunted the ATMs and filled my hotel room with euros that became more valuable by the hour. Space in nightstands and shelves became treasure troves of alcohol and food full of preservatives. This was by far the most expensive trip I'd ever taken, including the Irish fiasco. If we didn't find other accommodations soon we would run out of cash before Mother was cured or received palliative care. Neither scenario appealed to me: to become an orphaned street beggar or a benefit bum with his elderly, albeit unyielding, mother in tow. We both realized that this period had run its course. The very air we breathed was charged with a certainty that we had something new and unforeseen in store for us.

To stop the memories from evaporating into thin air I made one last big investment in a small electronic store on Kolverstraat. I bought a digital camcorder and gave it to Mother over our morning coffee one day in September, unaware that the world's data memory was in a more perilous state than it had ever been before the dawn of the digital age. Each and every hour was the predecessor of a memory that nuzzled in the bosom of eternity under the strong artistic direction of Mother. And so were our last days in Amsterdam: substantiation that we'd lived and enjoyed ourselves, downed specials and seen the Museum of Torture, because the ruthlessness of the past was such that everything was doomed to fade and vanish unless every moment was caught on film.

When I got a call from my credit card company complaining that the transaction for the camera should really not have gone through because of unpaid bills, there was nothing left to do but check out of Hotel Europa and cash in the insurance deposit. We decided to move to Lowland, stay at the guesthouse to begin with, and take it from there. I spent the last days roaming the streets, drinking coffee, buying books and music for smoother sailings into the future, whatever it was and however long it would last. We stood newly awake in the lobby with our luggage. A car horn honked out in the street. Amsterdam was behind us in the blink of an eye.

After a couple of days in Lowland it was as if we'd never lived anywhere else. Mother had a room on the ground floor and took her breakfast in the garden. Ramji would come pick her up at noon and drive her to get her shots from the doctor. Mastering her film, she made him walk seventeen times across the parking lot before his theatrical talent reached enough maturity to perfectly interpret the required casual spontaneity. Mother, on the other hand, only needed one take to deliver her most vital role. She insisted that I barbeque with Duncan to ensure that the memory of the wonderful festivities in Lowland would never be forgotten. The ritual involved drinking half a can of beer, stabbing a few holes into it and shoving it up the rear end of a dead chicken. Never before in the history of film-making had one bird been as thoroughly jammed. In this way Mother delivered the day-to-day life on Lowland complete and intact onto the pages of history—she being the only person I know of who managed to convince a cancer patient in a kilt to get down into a ditch and wave about a copy of *The Unbearable Lightness of Being*.

I was freer than I'd been for months and took over a room up in the attic on the south side of the guesthouse. I'd wake up to the morning sun, drifting in and out of sleep until noon, enjoying strange dreams about Ljudmila, the matron's daughter. Becoming closer to Duncan and his adventurous cooking resulted in my body expanding back to its old form, which made it possible for me, from a certain angle in the mirror, to imagine that my own ass was in fact Ljudmila's. That she'd snuck under my covers in the night and run amok.

Before the month was over Mother had moved into Highland, having secured a four-poster-bed and freestanding bath, like she'd dreamt of having on Spítala Street. Duncan offered to let her stay free of charge in one of the rental rooms; she had gone for a look, taken in the adventurously decorated lounges, the portraits, antiques, sewing machines, and chests. "And the garden, Trooper, what a paradise!" September passed with afternoon teas and blini parties. I couldn't help but think that the Fates had decided to be merciful. That she'd picked up the phone and consulted Joy. But it was too early to rejoice. At the end of the month one of Mother's bones snapped in two; she'd been directing Ramji while filming him changing a tire. After all these months, Mother had fallen ill.

*

When a parent loses a child the sorrow submerges the world; this was my first philosophical notion: if I died before Mother, the silence on Spítala Street would become an infinite abyss. Cousin Matti's record playing would never be able to fill it. The apartment would be flooded with tears, and no compensation for water damages could take away the pain.

Years later, in Dublin, when my self-pity reached full maturity, and the meaning of life poured out of my eyes and down my face, I tried to push on by reminding myself that despite everything there was a deeper sorrow, a sorrow that wipes out the significance of everything and reduces all the world's recordings to a chilling silence. I had friends who had suffered such a tragedy—people who'd buried their will to live along with their child, torn apart the frame of their existence, and said good-bye to each other; their life together meaningless without the child. Sorrow was a gravitational force dragging everything down into that grave. It could not be shared with others. It was reserved for them alone, beyond other people's understanding.

Soon after I split up with Zola I bumped into these unfortunate friends of mine in a restaurant in Dublin. They were back together again, had a new child and looked happy, sharing a meal. I, however, looked like an assembly of variously developed primates, unwashed and unshaved, in a blue suede jacket of Zola's, a very ugly and badly-cut piece of clothing that I'd grabbed on my way out after our last fight. My friends offered me a seat and delved into anecdotes from their lives, this great labyrinth of happiness that forced me, in my suede jacket, into the vast expanses of myself, overcome by the abyss. After my friends had sat under my non-stop, bearded ape's end-of-days rant for over half an hour, they'd had enough; it wasn't as if there were any children involved.

On my way over the mire separating Highland from the village, my mind was for some reason awash with a jumble of memories: dumped and dead-drunk in a Dublin hotel elevator; four years old hiding in a cupboard on Spítala Street, determined to stay there until my point had been made clear to Mother: that without me her life was worthless, that no matter how fun life was with grownups, without me it would never be more than an apparition. The longer I stayed in the cupboard the greater her happiness would be in finding me. She would not take off, she would not get sick, she would not die. The Spítala Street attic became a venue for adventures eliminating the danger of her ever going away. I appointed dusty household appliances as guardians from external attacks. I forbade her to go on summer vacation abroad with cousin Matti, on the grounds that I'd read in World Wonders that the Mediterranean was full of sharks. The years went by. One spring day brought on mutations of my organs. My voice broke. I had sexual relations with a badly upholstered Ottoman that smelled of dog biscuits. At the same time, Mother's presence in my life became unbearable.

She could never understand the catastrophes sweeping over my soul. My delicate body became a scene of spastic movements while my limbs grew and declared independence. I lost weight and put it back on. Each transformation was followed by new and unknown dimensions resonating through my psyche. The small corner shop became a palace of new feelings that embraced the summer nights and stretched out in the face of Pála, the shop assistant, who sold me gum and hot dogs. Night after night I went to meet her, sporting new additions to my face: blackheads and random stubble that resembled sparse pubic hair more than a beard. When I got back home I would dash up to the attic so *she* wouldn't be in my way. Cocoa Puffs became my *haute cuisine*. Meals were a thing of the past. Mother and I were no longer walking in line. Finally, I moved out. I began a new life were everything seemed possible, knowing little of what experiments the world had in mind for me.

Almost eighteen years had passed, but the fear of her death never quite left me. Deep down the child is still hiding in a closet, fixing up appliances in an attempt to prevent her death. We believe that experience works in our favor, that all the horrible moments and fuckups of our lives will give us perspective, but they don't. Adult life stumbles on-screen like a haze of meaningless jumble while the focus remains on the backdrop, distorting everything mounting up ahead. Sometimes the anxiety goes into hibernation and the set is ablaze with fantastic extravagance: drinking games, investments, and experimental intercourse with strangers. The havoc we wreak upon our own body makes sure no one ever suspects you to carry such primeval grief; that behind the calloused skin, guilt the size of a small child still survives. People tend to assume that a man who looks like that has experience enough to bury his childhood. But the closer I came to Highland, the heavier my steps were with the anxiety of seeing her so sick. It was a relief to see Ramji's Ambassador in the driveway with Frederik and Duncan huddling over the trunk.

"Willyson, my dear friend," the doctor called out and walked briskly toward me. "How splendid to have you here to see our patient. There are a few things we need to discuss now, the rest can wait. The Ukrain has failed. There is nothing we can do about that now. This is a tragedy for us all and especially for you, my dear friend. For you and your mother. There is no cure that can stop this train. All we have now is the morphine."

"How has she been today?"

"She's a fighter. If we're lucky she'll have many good days. A few weeks, even months. You never know with this disease. My gut tells me that we'll see sooner than later what to expect. This is the situation. We still have time to plan but we shouldn't leave it until it's too late."

"We came here to have this choice if it would come to this."

"Good, good." The doctor tapped a finger to his chin. "Well, there is something . . . do you know Dita van der Lingling? No? Dita was the first one to marry one of our patients. This was a long time ago. We don't really talk about it even though we sometimes find it handy. Tim Wallace died a married man. He died a Dutch citizen."

"Of course," I said, understanding where he was going with this. "And that's how you get around the euthanasia law?"

"Yes. I don't think we can send you to Switzerland. Duncan would never agree. I've given this a lot of thought and found a solution that suits everyone. Don't you agree, Hermann?"

I nodded my head and felt the strangeness of this all crawl over me, the grief that still was a distant shadow rather than a concrete feeling with consequence and meaning. We walked up the drive

and talked in more detail about the next steps, but then I said good-
bye and entered the building. The aroma of cooking and wine was
coming from the kitchen. The faint smell of autumn leaves seeped
through the open window in the lounge. Helena was nowhere to
be seen so I walked straight into the corridor leading to Mother's
bedroom. I didn't want to be there, not tonight. I wanted to run
back down to the gate, get into the car with the other men, drive
around Holland and return when Mother had been healed by a
miracle in the night. She would sit out on the lawn telling journal-
ists and reporters all about the wonder that erased the evil cells, like
the healing hand of Jesus, like the soothing touch of Buddha, and
the living cosmos blessing the steadfast. Walking into that room
was an act of duty that would only take a moment. I would pat her
on the back, disappear into the corridor and find Helena. Mother
would be better in the morning. Didn't Frederik say that you could
never tell with this disease?

I opened the door and took a seat next to the bed where she
lay sleeping. The Sphinx who had sat smoking on the balcony of
Hotel Europa with a glass of red wine and the stupendous beauty
of the night sky was gone. In its place was a drowned cat, the mane
wet with sweat and the body emaciated, beaten by the crashing
waves of the deep. I was seized by a vulnerability that seemed to
run through an invisible umbilical cord from her to me. The sedative effects of the morphine were ruthless to her face, making it
droop on the side she lay on, emphasizing the proximity of death.
I sat there trying to get used to it, trying on her illness, feeling the
weight of its smell and snoring, and didn't get up until my tremors
had subsided and my body had tuned into the confined stillness of
these circumstances that I knew would persist until the end. When
I stopped weeping I held her to me, absorbing her mumblings, tried

to swallow them like food and keep them down, scared of my gut, as if the party had been a hoax from the start, all the pork legs, the special drinks, all the joy that dozed off into dreams that were more beautiful than waking life. Because this was life, wasn't it? Life that didn't manifest in all its magnitude until the party was over?

"Hi, Trooper," Helena said when I walked into the lounge. She sat playing guitar, but put away the instrument and gave me a hug. "Did you go see her? Frederik says she needs rest. He's going to stay over tonight. He went with Duncan to Lowland to get his stuff."

"I know, I met them outside."

She got me a glass and poured me some white wine. I sat down, stood up again, took a deep breath by the window, and returned.

"I know how you feel," she said after a while. "I was just a kid when mom died but I totally understood what was going on. I know what it's like to watch your parent get sick."

"It's awful. To see her like that. Like she's been robbed of everything that makes her *her*."

"I don't know what it is about the illness that makes us so scared. You just don't want to face it. You want to run."

"But that's not an option. And then it's over, and you never quite get over it, do you?"

I told Helena that deep inside I had never believed Mother would get better. That everything would go back to normal and that we'd return home. But I didn't expect her to get so sick so soon.

"Maybe she knew for a while. Don't blame yourself. It's quite common for patients to cover up how bad it really is while they still can. But I'm really sorry, Trooper. Really. Even Frederik thought your mom had a chance."

We sat for a while and chatted until Helena said she had to return an amplifier she had borrowed from a neighboring farm. I was desperate to get out of the house and told her I'd join her and talk to Frederik in the morning.

"What about your mom?"

"They'll call me if anything changes. I'll be quick."

As we set out we saw Ramji coming up the driveway. It was getting dark. A cold breeze came across the meadow of the farm where we turned off the road onto a path cutting through the woods. A few pines grew in random formations among the deciduous trees that had succumbed to the fall. They were like chaperones at the orgy, life that clung to its existence in a world where everything was expiring. The earth was covered by a red and gold blanket, and aside from a lone bird answering the rustle of our footsteps, the woods were still. The setting sun cast little pools of light between the tree trunks, but it was cool and crisp in there, the sun rays cut the shadows with soft shards of light until it retreated and finally disappeared in the outskirts. It was the first time on the trip there I saw no buildings or traffic. For a moment it was as if a distant echo of the past had been blown our way, a reminder of how things had once been. Everything was exaggerated and illuminated in the dying light. I hadn't been out in nature for months and being suddenly surrounded by it sent an electric current surging through me.

"There's the farm," Helena said. "I don't want to stay. She's a bit cuckoo and won't stop talking if you let her invite you in. I'd much rather head back to Lowland and have a beer with you before I go back home."

She returned the amplifier and we walked back through the darkness. We sat for a while at the bar and then she left. I went to my room and lay there staring at the ceiling, counting the gnarls in the wood until I dozed off.

Chapter
17

I woke up late and was seized by an overpowering feebleness. After a brief struggle with a bottle of pills, I called Mother, who insisted that she didn't feel bad at all, that no living person enjoyed such luxuries as she did, and that the room service at Hotel Europa could not hold a torch to the pampering she was receiving from Helena and Duncan. Frederick would not have a flu-man near his cancer patients and was happy to agree when I suggested leaving Lowland while I got over the worst of it.

I decided to take a bus up north, let the gray landscape lull me to sleep and ease my mind. The dark gray clouds skated across the hemisphere. It was the kind of sky that could be painted any which way. As soon as the bus took off, the world became new, not Lowland, I glued my head to the window and disappeared into my thoughts. Both hemispheres of my brain displayed fireworks of long-gone cake and coffee parties, a fermented past wrapped in asparagus and ham, held up by Willy Nellyson's carved wooden cock. All this occupied my mind. I stared out the window. In Wormer, a squirrel hung straight out from a tree with pantyhose twisted around its feet; before he managed to free himself, the wind snatched at the nylon and the squirrel flew 10-12 feet before biting the dust. It was seriously windy. I felt as if I wasn't the only one who was at odds with reality. Outside, people were eating canned foods as if the Netherlands were the great disappointment in life, as if they'd come here from some former republic and thought that everything would be fine, but instead found a home on the side of the road. Everything was death. The phone wouldn't stop chirping text messages telling me that Iceland was on the highway to hell, that everything was lost and gone, that there was an exodus of private jets taking off with the goods before the country went bankrupt. I had given Iceland little thought in the past weeks and couldn't imagine that this was anything more than yet another circus act in the most pathetic play in history, starring Daniel Klambra. But the ATMs stood empty. The Bankers' Ball was over. A small wad of Króna notes was not worth much to the currency broker in Purmerend. I was penniless in a small town under sea level in a country I knew only a small corner of. I waited for the flood. A nap in a communal garden ended in an interrogation room at the police station where my passport was handled like a filthy magazine and I was treated like I was personally responsible for the greatest financial crisis to hit the area in modern times. The chief called his boss in Haarlem, the county capital, who confirmed his suspicions; if the man was Icelandic he should be incarcerated immediately. The entire savings of Holland had disappeared into the sewers of that nation. I suggested to the chief that they have a look in a golf lodge in Bulgaria, you just never know—they might just find some of those billions on the two Icelandic barbarians practicing their swing in the company of call-girls. I was told not to sleep in the train station but got permission to take a little nap out front while I waited for Helena to come and pick me up. She was alone. She was unhappy. Eila, her Faeroese girlfriend, had left her.

"I didn't know that you were gay," I said.

"Neither did I, not until I met Eila. I cursed and said fuck this, carpet muncher, fuck. But you know what? It's okay once you get used to it. The only drawback is watching the person you love shoving her tongue down someone else's throat. She took all the noise away, all the pain, all the useless shrink appointments, and I believed in her. I thought she was different from all the other people who've messed with my head. You can tell yourself that there are more fish in the sea. That you'll go on even though it seems impossible. But what if all the others won't do? You sit there with all your needs, all your misunderstandings and mess, until someone comes and kisses you and for the first time in your life you don't feel completely pathetic. What if you always get betrayed? What if life is nothing but one disappointment after another?"

"Then you just have a lifesaver and try to have fun." I took her in my arms and held her while she cried. I tried to console her by telling her anecdotes from my own life, that I didn't cry myself to sleep anymore over Zola, but that I believed that life had a paradox of endless possibilities. That one of these days maybe, in the future when your mind was clearer and you no longer limped across the surface of the earth like a stagnant form of the worst version of your dreams, then it would all come back, everything you'd lost, you'd get to love someone who smelled good, who always smelled of shampoo and who looked up every now and then from whatever she was doing and smiled if you were there. Because it just had to be, that somewhere in this sea of people wanting something completely different from what they had, there had to be someone who understood you, who understood your fragments, and I told her that I didn't see it often any more, I saw it rarely these days because there was darkness over the world. Mother was dying and I wanted to drown in my own tears, but I did see it once in a while, the possibility would fly through my mind and I'd feel slightly better, like now—I felt slightly better now.

"Is that why we do this? Because we think we can plaster up the holes? You could have let her die in Iceland, skipped the treatment, skipped it all. But you decided to come here. To be free when she left? To make up for something you feel is your fault?"

"I came to support her and because we can't do this sort of thing back home. I'm doing this because I have to, because it couldn't be avoided."

"It's so sad," she said. "They're both going to die and we'll never be able to forgive ourselves." She drove me to the city, passing by Lowland. I still had a few euros stashed away and wanted to get them out before they disappeared too.

"Make sure not to stay too long, Trooper," she said. "What ever you do in Amsterdam, don't forget why you came here. Promise me?"

"Promise," I said and gave her a little kiss on the mouth, but of course I knew I was lying.

*

My journey into the abyss started with a three-thousand euro annihilation at the post office. I took a taxi to Hotel Europa and checked into my old room, promptly emptied the minibar and rushed down to the lobby. The darkest, deepest sewers of the world were undefined dimensions awaiting me. The night was still collecting darkness. The city was overflowing with wine.

To commence my trip *en punto* I killed a row of shots from Dimitri and became instantly drunk, stumbled into the Red Light

170

District and found a strip bar, got a special drink called Apocalypse and watched two dancers perform nude ballet to Swan Lake. A topless stripper in a G-string asked if I'd buy her an Apocalypse but I told her that my apocalypse was a private affair, my time was reserved for drinking. I was going to explore the world's extent of hard liquors, the endless types and tastes, like a voyager who sets out to sea and sails without stopping. I was going to discover a new continent and become a pioneer, fight the beasts of the underworld until I died and was reborn, more powerful than ever before.

Out on the street corner, delicate movements in a mini skirt connected my brain to the past. It was Shaloo from Thailand who didn't do bondage sex and had once been a man. I was overcome by a sense of loss that catapulted me into her radius and the swaying of her skirt. If only the world still was a racist ball and a hangover, futility in tall glasses with the sound of laughter and denial. Then everything would be fine. Then nothing would be doomed. Her sleek, black hair was like background music in a soap commercial, her face bestowed with a symmetry that magnetized love of men, because this was femininity in all its glory, beauty that made men abandon reason and judgment, the very foundations of existence, until the mess took over, everything fell apart, the core was ripped out and torn to pieces, marriage, family, and day-to-day life.

"Shaloo!"

She turned around, looked right through me and stared for a while as if all the triviality of the world was embodied in me. As soon as she turned away the insanity of my outburst crept into my soul and I took off in the other direction. It didn't matter how much this raised me on Mother's Gay Scale in other ways than to show how delusional I had become. Three men in a rubber speedboat brought home the fact by spraying me with foul canal water. My sorrow deepened, death and darkness took hold of me. Half awake, half with my senses drenched in Zodiac-waste, I walked aimlessly toward Achterburg, where the prostitutes posed in the windows. My mind fluttered to the possibilities of taking part. A short visit to a world where all men were animals and dragons convulsing in proportion to the mistakes they were capable of making. Not to think of what Zola said about sex with hookers. Rather think about Daniel Klambra. He did this. He never noticed the world sinking into the mud. His mouth didn't fill with sand. The fog didn't creep in. Darkness didn't fall. I could do this. Just carry on and don't think, seize the moment and *go for it!*

I'd walked past five to six windows with beautiful girls in their twenties before finally bolting like a man under fire into a dimly lit first-floor room where a chubby, tired looking woman stuck her tongue out at me. Her shabby, plump body ground on top of me, lying half-naked in this pocket of time, the moment it took for me to undress and, short of breath, tell her about my life, the loneliness and the beauty, until I realized I was incapable of sex and she told me not to worry, this happened all the time, I could watch her while I jerked off or talked, I had fifteen minutes left on the clock and was free to do with them as I pleased.

In order to forget this incident as soon as possible, I decided to go and find Steven at the Cannabis Museum, take a hit from the bong and embrace my depression. But Steven wasn't there, the museum was closed, and no one I knew was on Warmoestraat. My only interaction with the world was to silence my constantly ringing phone. Helena called, as did Duncan, Helga, and finally the doctor—but I couldn't answer. The squall of phone calls receded into a number of bobbing text messages I didn't read or understand.

Mountain Lady? Democracy Baby? As long as I ignored this, the world would stand still. As long as there was silence, everything was okay.

I was blitzed by the time I reached Chinatown, where I bought a spring roll, found a whisky bar, and forgot about time, drifting as far away as I possibly could from all that concerned me: the disease, morality, and my role in this farce called life, in its constant proximity to death, ever drawing near. Because everything disappeared and receded, everything grew dark and the day crawled toward the night. I had to take the power back. I had to wipe out the meaning by ending this. Don't quit now. That would be a betrayal to the pain. I had to cross the ocean that changed me. This was a war with futility and frivolity. I had to drink until I dropped dead.

That's how my first day went. I drank and told myself not to eat until someone found me in the gutter and force-fed me solids with a funnel. I ate the sky for breakfast, digesting the stars before lunch. For dessert: a bottle of Veuve Clicquot and a foot-long row of tequila shots. Dawn poured out of me and flowed into the gutter with the night. I threw up between car bumpers that exchanged information about my soul. I was Timothy Wallace before reason reached his ears. Mother before her first AA meeting. The world with a broken heart. All those who'd ever tried to destroy their own life with alcohol.

After three days the exercise had just about delivered me to my goal. I was in no shape to survive the day without pouring more alcohol into my body. Immediately, my mind disappeared into slurred hallucinations that howled at me with the same lack of pitch as the herds of English girls roaming the city's karaoke bars in little hen parties. Mother was the hen and Death her groom, flying together into eternity. I sang along, having forgotten the lyrics, lost my party and everyone in it, and I snored loudly when I was unconscious, at least that was what the hotel maid told me with her compassionate expressions and questions about difficult nights. As soon as she left I jumped across the room, attacked the reloaded minibar and ventured out into the daylight on the wings of newly drunk beers. The messages kept coming, so did the phone calls. *Where are you, Trooper? We need to get a hold of you.* My eyes stole a peek at the screen in a fit of early morning forgetfulness, but then I remembered I mustn't read them. *The room is welling up with wailing* . . . I threw the phone into the next trashcan. My lungs dissolved into the drumbeats of the coffee shops. Mother had to be dead by now, coffined, incinerated, or in the ground already. Anywhere but here with me, I was everywhere but with her. Because I had run off. I kept on running away, as far as I could into the night.

And so a week passed in Hotel Europa with random visits to the gutter. Finally I broke. I broke the string of the bow that quivered in my heart with all its arrows. I howled into a nauseating vacuum and screamed at it, fraught with helplessness and self-pity over all the things I would never be able to make up for or fix, a cumulative nervous breakdown of all these months and weeks. I'd come to do good, to do everything I could for Mother and attempt to put right all that had gone wrong, polish away all the smut of yesteryears' Christmases, whisper silence over the screaming that preserved the suffering and pain. We were supposed to believe, when all was said and done, that we'd never been ill in the soul, that we'd never thrust daggers into each other's hearts and twisted them in the wounds, laughing about it, that we'd never pretended like nothing was wrong. Mistakes were like new grass in spring, mowed down and filling the world with the most beautiful fragrance there is. That was how the memory would be when everything that created it was put together. We lay there in the grass with white-wine spritzers, foie gras, and this memory, and a good day, and our dreams. Daylight like it had been sieved through the darkness of the soul, new again to us.

Now the scene was crumbled, grinning ghoulishly at me. Bits and pieces strewn all over like flotsam and jetsam. The wind pushed me down into the dirt and I whimpered. I broke down. It was over, I had fucked up. Like everything else in my life, I had fucked up, I'd taken on this journey and gutted it, ripped it apart in the final lap to ensure that Mother went crying into her grave, so that my life would always be this raging storm and I would have to live with this anxiety, unhappiness, and the resolution that would never be.

Barely conscious, half asleep on the bathroom floor, I rose to my feet when I heard shuffling from the door that penetrated my nightmare. The room was a maelstrom of light, full of things flying into a screaming silence. I felt for painkillers in the bathroom cabinet, washed them down with a large bottle of water from the minibar, paused in front of the door and listened. Then I opened it.

"Here you are! Duncan and I have been looking all over for you! Oh, Trooper!" Helena followed the stench of ethanol secreting from my body and gently patted my head as I let it hang over the side of the bed. "Eva was asking for you. She went on and on about some mountain lady and cried over not being the child of the republic or something we didn't understand. Democracy Baby? She said it over and over."

"Is she dead?" I asked.

"No, Trooper . . . she's not dead! We needed to get a hold of you because she and Duncan decided to get married."

I looked up with two black holes for eyes, caught in a debate with comprehension.

"I was thrilled to marry Eva," Duncan said, "even though the reason was a matter of convenience."

"You got married? You've actually had a wedding?"

"We need to make sure the citizenship goes through in time. We just didn't get what she meant with not being Icelandic anymore, not being a mountain woman. She cried so much. She didn't want to do this without you."

I felt the tears well up in my eyes and Helena's hands on my face, bloated and cried out, until she held me tight, looked into my eyes, and hugged me. "Come with us, Trooper. Okay? Everything is going to be fine. Please, come with us and finish what you came here to do."

"Yup, yes," I started, but my voice was unstable, a quivering needle on a seismograph preparing for an explosion, wanting to explode. "I just needed some rest," I tried to say but couldn't. I gasped for breath in the presence of these people who I had just recently learned to know. I felt like I needed to pull myself together in front of them, maintain the mask we insist on calling self-respect when the truth is we're all broken underneath it, full of repressed angst and neuroticism that inflates like a balloon until it explodes and drives us over the edge, our insides spilling out into the world like a Biblical torrent, a liberating force turning you into a baby, crying uncontrollably and passionately. "I was on my way . . ." I bawled, crying like a kid who's been caught eating all the popsicles in the freezer, all the cookies in the attic, and all the soda in the pantry.

"I know it's not easy, son," Duncan said, infusing my weeping with a warmth that only served to heighten my hysteria, so I fell completely silent, choking on my own crying, keeling over, overwrought by sobs. My lungs were about to explode into Duncan's kind face staring down at mine, distorted by lament, threatening to rip my expressions apart, peeling away my skin, red like the furious flames of Hell. He placed a hand on my shoulder and looked at me with that gentle Santa Claus look, which had to be what all living creatures would like to see in their dying breath, all those hung over and dejected, because it wiped away fear, brought pure tranquility to all things, and calmed the heart so that all did not seem lost anymore: nothing was completely impossible if you just managed to pull yourself together.

"We understand this has not been easy for you. I know it and my Helena knows it. That's why she's coming back to Highland, to help out. Don't you think it's best that you come and see Eva, too? We'll cook something good to get the poison out of your system. I know the state you're in, I've been there numerous times myself, and I suppose your mother knows it too. She's just waiting for you to return."

I slept in Helena's room that night, in her double bed in Lowland. The sheets were drenched from sweat and spit and the cold cloths Helena used to wash my face while I tossed and turned, and she stayed awake telling me stories from her life, trips to the Faroe Islands, and her love for Eila. Eila whom she'd get over, Eila who would be a gauge for the past, Eila who would no longer be sadness, but a new beginning. Because there was light up ahead. There would be still mornings and dawns that would wake us with a vastness enabling us to take on life. When I came to, the morning was my negative—bright and high—I gaped at it, crazed by the emptiness echoing in my head, carried on the shoulders of the horror and pain in my body as if the world had defecated on me, made me a gutter for all the shit oozing out of its endlessness, and yet promised to return me to the purging light. Because there was still hope after all. A sliver of hope, despite everything, to fix what had been broken.

Chapter
18

Even the most spectacular hangover can't dull the panic of suddenly being poor. I would have lost myself in the vacuum, disappeared down a bag full of chocolate and the complete collection of *Liebe Sunde* if the situation had just been the aftermath of heavy drinking. But as I walked over to the Mansion at the crack of dawn with my head full of the online news about the disaster in Iceland, so infinitely worse than any message in Haarlem had conveyed, I was seized by such anguish over the future that I wanted to run to the woods, evaporate into the canopy, and not return until the world was new again. It wasn't the fact that Iceland was down, the banks busted, and the Prime Minister had resorted to asking for God's blessing for the country as it tanked, but the thought of having Mother's illness to deal with and no money to do so was something I hadn't prepared for. I'd eaten the last euro in the form of a sandwich during the trip from Amsterdam to Lowland. I was no longer a stranger to the world's deepest and darkest cesspools. We had pushed aside all hindrances to agitation and anxiousness, and laid down in the dirt. Now we'd bury our sorrows by heading penniless into the future.

I found little comfort in the fact that this catastrophe was not mine alone. The governor of Holland claimed to have transferred one hundred and twenty thousand Icelandic documents and files to the Bank of Holland that had turned out to be devoid of all significance and meaning. This pressed tree pulp from the North-Atlantic would be best used for ass-wiping as it was of no use as currency in places of business. The savings were lost. The Bank of Holland had hired sixty experts to sort through the paperwork on the second floor of the bank's HQ on Westeinde, but had to relocate the operation because the building couldn't support the weight of the great bulk of paper. Never before in the history of civilization had people fled their houses on account of paper. Iceland was subjected to anti-terrorist legislation, thus joining a list including al-Qaeda and North Korea. In my inner world the lists were reserved for the adventures of my hangovers. I was not at all sure how long I would survive as I crawled up the steps to the old mansion.

Dr. Fred welcomed me in his green coat, ready with a saline drip and vitamin remedy. He told me I just needed to lie down while the solution trickled through and replenished my stores. That left the more serious and pressing matter of the relentless itching around my genitals. The good doctor whipped out his magnifying glass and let out a delighted cry. *Pthirus pubis pacificus!* If he was not mistaken this was one of the rarest genus of crabs in the Netherlands, known to have been originally transmitted by Dita van der Lingling.

"Are you implying that I had sex with Dita van der Lingling?"

"Well, the little buggers may have claimed a larger territory in the past few years, but for the longest time they could almost always be traced back to Dita. She has a man in the Pacific. It's a peculiar world, the sex industry."

"No shit."

Dr. Fred assured me that there was no need for drastic measures, all I needed was to rub a bit of Permetrine on the area and wash all clothing that may had been in contact with Petirus.

"By the way, your name has come up quite a lot this morning," he said.

"Oh?" I felt my heart break because I was sure I knew what was coming.

"Because of that bank that Helga wanted to deposit our savings into," he continued and my apprehension grew. "Wasn't it run by your compatriots? Well, Helga tells me that it's all gone to hell, and therefore we count ourselves extremely lucky that you warned us about it. The savings in Lowland are nothing to brag about but at least they are here, safe and sound."

*

Mother wasn't angry when I showed up again. She reached out to me and smiled, asked me to sit with her, patted her eiderdown and squeezed my arm.

"I didn't mean to be gone so long," I started. "I just . . ."

"No need to apologize, love, Duncan has been such a blast while you were away. Did they tell you we got married? I never imagined I'd get married so late in life."

"Duncan's lucky to have found himself such a wife."

"And so am I, Trooper, so am I."

"I'm sorry I wasn't with you."

"We'll find time to drink to that—don't you worry. There are still things to celebrate here in Lowland even though Iceland is upended. I got a letter from cousin Matti. Apparently everything is crazy back home, have you heard? No culture and endless money cults, like I've always said. We were lucky to get out in time." She gently pinched my cheek. "You look a bit groggy . . . you kind of remind me of a Munch."

"A monk?"

"Edvard Munch, the grand master painter of the soul. You kind of look like one of his paintings, just duller—more gray."

I had a hard time keeping what had happened from Mother and ended up telling her everything that I'd been through, my drinking in Amsterdam, days I spent with me and myself, my dallying with the sordid side of life and the abyss. The fact was that there aren't many people who can listen as intently to other people's tales of woe as Mother. Her take on the matter was that I'd taken one for the team and was in fact ecstatic that my excursion—this testament to our stay in Amsterdam—had ended in the arms of a prostitute.

"Ran out on her fully clothed and yet you managed to get crabs!" She howled with laughter. "Just like your dad, in and out of whorehouses with his pants around his heels. It's just in your DNA. I mean, what else have you been doing out at night, all by yourself, if not roaming the Red District? I was sure you were out there getting your rocks off."

I couldn't help but laugh and we sniggered together for a while until I had to get back to Lowland to tend to my hangover. It was a mammoth task, but one at which I was determined to succeed. I was, after all, an expert when it came to the aftermath of drinking, fully schooled in the psychological and cultural aspects of it. Crippled offspring ambushed my dreams like deformed flakes: somehow me, but child sized, and with abscesses everywhere. Screaming, wolf-faced women in the inner most circle of Hell, mid-coitus. Above the haze a starlit canopy shimmered, pressing into my eyelids and shaking me. I had rarely been so harassed as these nights when I tossed and turned, trembling from going cold turkey. All the sleepless nights, the fits and sweat. When it came to hangovers, I was king. When it came to hangovers, I was Edvard Munch, grand master painter of the soul.

In the end the colors stopped burning and everything became gray and lumpy like a porridge of surroundings, blowing leaves, and raindrops falling down my back. The tone scale was a silent bass reminding me of the couple of minutes before Christmas, the moment when all went still, even the radio. I told myself that I would never drink another drop of alcohol. That it was not for me, but for people like Duncan and Mother who knew how to handle it, understood its many dimensions and uses. From now on I would deal with my anxieties without resorting to alcohol. Nothing was of any importance except Mother's illness.

I continued to surf the Internet and sank deeper each day into the disaster unfolding in Iceland. The misery bled into my grief over the illness, and the fusion reached completion in a story I found on a website with the heading *Icelandic Woman Ends Her Own Life in Hospice Abroad*. I stared at the screen, overcome with sadness because we had told no one of our plan. No one but cousin Matti, who would never have gone to the papers. Farther down the page was a link to *related articles*. I clicked the link and saw the face of Danni Klambra spread over the screen. He smiled his white-toothed grin underneath text about Vikings, Iceland booming, Fixrenta conquering the buy-to-rent market, Bulgaria being silicon, there you could live the high life, but the Netherlands was the place to be if you wanted to enjoy your final days, Icelanders went there for medical care, there was an Icelandic woman there receiving palliative care, didn't that tell you something about the quality of Fixrenta's services in the Netherlands? *It's even nice to die here.*

The article had been published a few days before the Klambra boys went under. Since then the reporter had managed to dig up our names and published a photo of Spítala Street 11. The house had been sprayed: *Blasphemist, Suicide is a crime.* A spokesperson from a Christian sect felt the need to defend the defiling of the house while others defended Mother. People with wooly hats and mittens in colorful clothing stood in front of Spítala Street with a signs saying: *One Life—One Choice! God is Dead! Eva's Choice!*

I called Matti who said he had tried to phone me. The situation had spiraled quickly out of control. People stood out there in the cold in support of Mother. Protests were taking place all over the city center, cars were set on fire and politicians didn't leave the house without bodyguards to protect them from the Public's accusations of treason.

"Are all these people protesting because of me?" Mother asked, looking over my shoulder at the protest on screen. For a second I almost gave in to the truth, to tell her that Iceland had fallen, had sunk into the Atlantic. The people standing there were the people who couldn't get a ticket out of there. People who never had private planes at their command, no condos in Bulgaria. That these were the single moms with their rolling pins and pans, the eczema-plagued children longing for zinc cream, the dogs needing flea shampoo and Pedigree, the IceTaxi people demanding justice, the street people suffering from soaring wine prices, guitar people in need of amplifiers, people who solve puzzles in Excel, people who want vitamins for their children, teenagers wanting DVDs, the elderly needing meds, and the whole nation wanting to reclaim its country after the bombardment and self-jets. All the commies, Mother, all the commies! But I didn't want to hurt her. Why couldn't these people just as well be protesting because of Mother?

184

"Well, I never thought I'd become this famous. Imagine, all these people standing there thinking of me. I feel a bit like I did in Montparnasse back in the day. I think I'll have a glass of red and a cigarette. I feel much better now."

I gave her a light, wiped the sweat off her forehead and the toxins oozing out through her skin producing that distinct whiff of illness, the heavy odor constantly reminding us of death. She was like a tiny chemical plant, the smoke like a tiny factory cloud over a building that was falling apart. I didn't know what went on in there, what kind of sound travelled in a house doomed to fall, but it was more than crying. Music, long-gone parties, drives up mountainsides, and adventures, this was the hint of happiness that constantly flickered up ahead and made the point apparent, even though the hand never quite grasped what it was reaching for. Mother participated in order to collect memories, enjoyed in order to feel the loss, and even though reality tormented her and ordered her to bed, she possessed a serenity that I had a hard time defining as surrender.

And yet I could no longer ignore what was happening. I could no longer pretend not to see that which demanded my full attention; the pain that burned through Mother's bones, the agony that made her cry and shout at me that she wanted to do it now, drink acid or anything that would make her disappear from the face off the earth. She could drink moonshine, like the stuff that killed Grímur, Great Aunt Edda's father, first by blinding him and then by burning a hole in his stomach. She would do it. Anything but this. We knew the end was drawing near. We could not postpone this much longer. Even though the heart calmed down and the pain receded, it was always looming. Always returning, until she died. Until she faded and disappeared. She was pain. She was a distorted face and the hate for that which distorted it.

That was how the week after my return from the abyss in Amsterdam passed. All I could do was wipe away her tears and sweat, administer morphine and wait for the party to be over, for the constant rave-hopping of the mutated cells to stop. Sometimes she would ask Duncan to lie down beside her, he told such wonderful stories, possessed a kindness that was more important than muscles and chest hair, and even though it had taken cancer and old age for her to learn this lesson . . . was it maybe always meant to end like this? Until now there had been no Duncan. We knew that the time they had together was limited, full of hindrances and howling into the silences, suffering that chewed up the darkness and set the room on fire without notice. It grew colder and Mother got worse. She didn't say much, filling her presence with something that was the negative of who she was, as if life was sucking out everything that made her herself. Duncan said that when people stopped crying over their own past it finally became the past, insignificant and useless, no longer a thing to measure life against, no longer a tool for evaluating everything you wanted back, only that which has passed. At the same time you felt the weakness that made you give up. Like Mother, he was dying. He had about three months left, maybe less.

Mother told me to keep a record. Told me that I should tear out the pages of her journal and eat them if that helped me make any sense of them. Life was one big crime novel and it had to be put into words. The bombardments of the self-jetters should be recorded. The torture of patients in modern times was a vital topic to write about, for outdated injection techniques did nothing but make you want to kill yourself as soon as possible. But there was also joy in the world that needed mentioning as well. Hotel Europa had to live on in the minds of others, the breakfasts and the shopping trips, all the museums we visited with her lifesaver in hand, that wonderful companion, and Timothy and Duncan had to be mentioned, never forget how much fun there is to be had, drink some calamus in a crazy jazz orgy and dance. In between all of this her own personality would achieve immortality, the best height of imagination when all was said and done, even though the world was too dumb to appreciate it.

November brought rain and the rotten fall engulfed everything. The smell of decomposing leaves stroked the plains, the wind picked up, and the last of the summer flowers yielded to the ground. If Mother perked up, the delight only lasted a short while. She raged at the changing of the seasons and this inexplicable life. The days with Duncan became memories, empty glasses, forgotten embraces on the lawn, and nothing could change the fact that everything was lost. I watched her face break and the corners of her mouth droop toward the trail of death. She shouted away the squirrels in the meadow and screamed the knots out of the wind so the country-side went completely still, and then she instantly fell in love with the world again. She praised my calm temperament, reached for my hand; a skeleton craving water, flesh and blood, broke down and got angry with herself. Maybe the look of hate is most potent when it is directed inwardly. Sometimes her expressions betrayed an unbearable regret of not having done things differently. She cried over the injustice she had thoughtlessly caused me, inconsolable over mistakes that threw happiness out with the trash. She mourn-ed disposable opportunities and unrecyclable pleasures, a forgotten birthday. When she was haunted by thoughts of all the things she hadn't done, painting lessons, suing the conservatives for treason, it was like all the days of history wouldn't suffice to grieve over what would never be. Life was a wreck no matter how long it was. She had never enjoyed any of it. Existence was a merciless narrow path to damnation and hell. She hated it. She hated existence and all its ruined days more that her own useless bones.

When she came to, she remembered where she was and that most of this was over and done with, long forgotten and that everything else was more important—to rest her feet for half an hour in Duncan's lap and sleep—and at such moments joy settled over everything around Highland. The grass was glad to die underneath the frost. The cattle happily chewed on the wire fences. Fantasy and wonder skated hand in hand over her features, like a drunken couple that has always loved each other, but never fully understood the other. In her blood was a tremor she considered a betrayal of happiness, and it was that very tremor that called the whole world to its service and attracted people who gave her their love. I read to her and she fell asleep listening, woke up wanting cotton candy, maybe a *Liebe Sunde*, some Icelandic flatbread with onion pâté. She babbled on and on, salivating at the mouth, her voice rattling, black, white, black, white, black: her consciousness flickered, moving in and out of existence without any discernable rhythm. Events swirled out of control in her mind, constantly on repeat. Everything was new, even things that had happened before, so the reverberation of progress didn't intensify the monotony but rather hampered it. Each hour was the last, but also the first, a constant recurrence of the eccentricity of the disease. Sometimes she would recognize the beauty by cursing the lack of jenever, but I knew she didn't have the stomach for it anymore, and that was all I knew. Her mortality was beyond everything that my mind could perceive, but each time it hit me I was overwhelmed by sorrow and obsessed with a need to be especially kind to her. I craved confirmation of this one thing more than anything else: that I'd done everything in my power. No matter how deep the sorrows, there had been someone ready to appease them. And that she would say it: You did good, Trooper. Better than anyone else.

My worst fear was to live with the possibility of having failed her. I convinced myself that death justified everything, framed everything, and if we did it right the doubts would never haunt me again. Helena was in the same situation. She led Duncan through the days, tried to support him, tried not to break under the pressure from unfair feelings belting drinking songs from the deepest corners of her soul, convincing her that she had failed. Because there is only so much you can do. The roads that people traveled were many, long, and different. Not everyone came to the same crossroads at the end of the road.

"Don't think you failed, Trooper, just because other people think differently."

But it didn't change anything. I was pulled north and south by delusions cooked up by a cocktail of medications and temperament—if I showed signs of weariness it hurt and sometimes I would cry in the woods, feeling the cold of the last, falling leaves up against my face. I smelled the earth and the cold fall dissolving the ice and threading the wetness underneath me while Mother shrank and withered away. She disappeared like the breeze into silence. For the first time in my life I heard her say things only old people say. Last spring felt like the next World War, so far away that you could reminisce about it in a meaningless void. I tried to leave the house as little as possible, sitting in the windowsills looking out at the grass and the animals. Golden thorns grew in sinewy wisps of cloud. Inside of me was a sadness I had never experienced before.

Chapter
19

"We need to start taking measures," the doctor said. "Nothing but the equalizer will do from now on."

He handed me an IV bag with a long tube to attach to a catheter. People couldn't handle the drip for long, he said, the side effects would start kicking in after a couple of weeks, but for a short while it was a wonder drug. Frederik had developed the concoction after decades of research, calculating the right value of the phenethylamines in proportion to the opiates.

"And people seem to hang on to their personality pretty well," he said. "Thanks to those like Tim Wallace; there would be no equalizer without them. Some professionals insist that it disorients that patient, but that's not my experience. Your mother is in severe pain and it's only going to get worse. When the sarcoma gains the upper hand it tends to be more painful than other forms of cancer. We'll need to play it by ear. It's just a question of time now."

"I'll see if I can't convince her," I said. "I won't run away again, Frederik. Promise."

"Good. Good."

We said good-bye and I headed back to Highland, past a crowd of people with loudspeakers and signs. Arthur van Österich was going to die tonight and there were some protests to be expected. Most of the commotion was thought to be around Lowland so the grounds had been closed off. Dozens of people stood out by the road shouting slogans, life above all, no one shall decide another person's death.

"I understand it's like this around all the hospices in the country," Helena said when I met her in the lobby. "These people actually make the special trip up here to cause a racket, as if there isn't enough shit going on to scream about. We go to war, spend our tax money on warfare, the oldest pact in the world that it's okay to take a human life when that's the way the wind blows. And still those bastards show up here and shout at us as if we're criminals." This was not the first time I'd heard her rant about the opponents of euthanasia, and she hadn't finished: "People think it's fine to watch others disintegrate. They don't do anything about people dying like dogs in the street. But if those same people decide to throw themselves off a bridge they're accused of taking into their hands a power that's not theirs. People don't stand out there in the cold protesting because they care, but because we take away their illusions. We take away the optimism and abundance by acknowledging death."

"Maybe some people just have stronger beliefs than others," I said, not understanding why I felt the need to defend them.

"I think you're just saying that because you're scared now. I sometimes think the same way, that maybe Duncan will live long enough to survive this, if he decides not to take his own life. That he could die in slow motion so I can lie to myself, tell myself that death is not horrible, that it is something completely different, but I know that he's had enough. People don't think about that when they show up here with their signs. Their opposition doesn't come from compassion, but out of rage. They think those who commit suicide are committing a crime against everyone they leave behind, but then they don't care about people dying because of poverty. People don't care about the next guy as long as he doesn't kill himself."

I wanted to agree with her, give some philosophical input on our situation, this world that championed the freedom of the individual to such an extent that he could ruin a whole nation by photocopying documents, but then object to Mother getting help in dying. However, I had not grown up with this idea like Helena had. She saw that and asked me to excuse her lecturing, she just couldn't contain her indignation sometimes.

"No worries," I said. "I understand you too. People sometimes think it's easier to correct other people's lives instead of their own."

"Which is why they go into psychology," she replied. "Or take short cuts by shouting and waving signs. But in the end we all have to face ourselves."

"I suppose so. I think it's best that I go see what she wants to do about the drip."

I walked into the room and sat on the bed. It didn't take much to convince Mother to agree to the equalizer. Each drip counted down the days we had left. The mornings imported sense to remember all our victories in Amsterdam in the beginning of summer, when all days were special drinks and delight. That was life, that was the memory. We moved furniture around to make better use of the living room and made Highland a theatrical stage for the past. Ramji got movers to bring in a hospital bed on wheels. I got out the photographs we'd taken with us from home, scanned them into the computer and held slideshows in the dining room. Duncan slept a lot; Mother and I were mostly alone with the hundreds of photos, each telling a story. Reykjavik. Berlin. Montparnasse. When Willy Nellyson lit up the wall she said: "He had his good points, your dad." The balcony of Hotel Europa got a more enthusiastic reaction. The Amstel river and everything we'd done: Trooper in de Dam in Rembrandtplein, Trooper sleepy after the single glass of wine.

"Lord, we've had fun," she said, flipping through a series of cousin Matti having a banana smoothie that was so well documented it looked like a moving picture. "Do you remember, Trooper? When all days were drinking days, and the weekends too?"

I could recall being confined to the attic with a pound of chocolate and *E.T.* on full blast to drown the revelry downstairs.

"There was singing and laughing back then. Do you remember Brownie? Completely bonkers, but the funniest person I've ever met. She passed out on our Moscow trip and never woke up again. But she lived while she lived."

I was transported back in time and was once again hit hard by the inevitability of the end. Each passing moment is the last, each day goes by for the last time. And the days were becoming fewer. The moment had come for her to decide how she wanted to die. Did she want to breathe in nitrogen? Helium or argon? Or did she want to drink barbital, which was what Arthur van Österich chose to do in the end? His death was described as peaceful and painless in all of the major papers. I cut out his last statement from one of them and translated for Mother:

> *Nothing can prepare you for the fear that grips you at death's door. My life's work has been to convince people to have the courage to accept their fate without fear or falsehood. I've maintained that with the right preparations each and*

everyone can choose their final hour and live it without fal-
tering, close their eyes for the last time without regret. These
past few days I've been both restless and scared. I judge no
one for their choice of path, whatever it is and whatever it
entails, as long as it causes no harm to others. Respectfully
yours, Arthur van Österich.

The fear set on Mother like a storm from within her bones. After a couple of days on the equalizer the world became such a pleasure dome that it was inconceivable that the darkness would ever return. Free of the constant invasions of the physical world, the Sphinx in her rose again and she became more prophetic than any tarot card, righteous, lucid, undaunted, noble and celestial in spirit, as if the pillars of the earth had merged with her feet. With faith in this equanimity she pulled out the drip and was almost instantly overcome with blinding angst. In the half hour this hurricane swept over her she hated death more than all the disappointments life had brought her. She felt it in the pain that ripped her humanity away, turning her into a reptile and a harpy, and yet she would not let go, didn't want to die. No matter how death tried to seduce her with promises of rest, peace, eternal sleep in the embrace of the stars where her light shone on the world and the sky is the reflection of Eva Briem, she would not go. Anything was better than to disappear and become nothing but this deafening, terrible silence, this gaping void around a body that is doomed to rot, become a skeleton, dirt, and dust. The ache dug into her marrow and rammed a hot poker into her spine for the eleven thousand hours that half hour without the equalizer seemed to last. To live and then suddenly no longer exist: this journey from one level of existence to another brought a crazed dimension of fear. The reverse side of sixty years of experience flickered on in a second, but what did it contain?

I tried to tell her that she would always exist, in my mind and Helena's, in cousin Matti's heart, and Duncan's and in everyone who had ever touched this grindstone, the people protesting her death in Iceland and in those who supported her all the way, who would stand by her when the final hour came. I told her that she was heroic, all the grand master painters of the soul rolled into one. I gave every speech you think will salvage something when the seas are calm, when the distant possibility of death is just a possibility, just fantasy on a summer's day because death is a part of life, the autumn leaves fall, the seasons change, and we know that somewhere beyond all of this are longer days where the silence calls out to us, but all this time the idea is unreal in its remoteness. We say these things to give us courage, to console those leaving before us, claiming that we never stop being our works and actions, that which we leave behind with our loved ones for them to keep till the end of days. But this idea is shit. Because when all is said and done, nothing will make us reconciled with death.

I sensed that Helena was having a hard time so I held her in silence. We moved closer to each other than could be constrained by daywear. Desperation creates hollows in the labyrinth of the brain that don't require intoxication to fill, just anguish.

"I just get lonely and then I don't want you to leave."

"I don't want to leave."

"So don't leave. You can hold me, just for a while, because you're you."

I was completely lucid, I'd never ventured through the days with such sobriety. The high I experienced was the undiluted reality, the dripless existence that I knew Mother would never experience again.

It was well into December when we finally convened in the kitchen to go over the paperwork. Helena made tea, Duncan and Mother lay together on the couch, Frederik handed out the papers. I filmed her signing her name with an unstable hand. It had to be crystal clear that no one was making this decision for Eva Briem Thórarinsdóttir. She was the one letting go of the spark, the longing that was ignited of the very certainty that she had to die. Even Frederik, who had been in this situation numerous times, helped hundreds of patients down this painful path, let the scientist's mask fall for a moment, giving our hands a quick squeeze under the soft kitchen light. We knew this was the end. She would be dead within a fortnight.

"I'm going to drink barbital," she finally said and handed him the document. "I'll drink barbital on New Years Day and that will be that."

Chapter
20

A t the break of dawn on the day of the wedding I walked alone across the snow-covered cemetery and sat down by her plot. A grayish owl circled over the field that would become Mother's last resting place. She chose the spot herself, a quiet corner at the edge of the already overcrowded old cemetery, under a large maple tree. She said her heart would always belong to Iceland, but her remains would find rest here, in Lowland's cemetery where the road ended.

I walked back to the church and counted my steps as they dug into the ground. The blankness all around exaggerated this intimacy with my surroundings: documenting each detail, constantly registering reality to memory before my world would disintegrate and disappear. The night had dressed the countryside in white as fitted the occasion, and the air was crisp from melting ice that drip-dropped on the church steps. It was pleasant to step inside the warmth. Steven sat in the antechamber drinking coffee and dressed in a corduroy suit. He was back to his lanky old self, stick thin like the day I had first met him. BodySnatch was now owned by a large corporation. He and Gloria had bought a penthouse in the center of Amsterdam with the profits and donated the rest of the money to Libertas. He pushed a cup of coffee toward me and asked me to have a sip, give it a minute, and then have another.

"First hot, then cold?" he asked and I nodded. "I don't know what's inside these thermoses that keeps the coffee hot all day long, but as soon as it's in the cup it gets colder much faster than newly brewed coffee. This must be coffee from yesterday. Monica probably couldn't be bothered to make a fresh pot this morning so it immediately pisses out all heat."

"Unless it's a matter of the coffee pissing into the cup and then pissing off," I said. "Then all you've got left is piss, no coffee."

"That'll be it—piss. I'm throwing this out."

As soon as he got to his feet Helena came in wearing a light blue dress and high heels with golden swans on the sides. I asked if her secret mission to hide all contours of her body was over, but she just smiled and took me by the hand, leading me outside. She said she had made up her mind.

"I'm going back to med school, right after the holidays. If I do well Fred's going to train me as his successor."

"That's great news."

"It just dawned on me how absurd it was to ruin all my chances just because I was afraid of becoming a cliché. I thought that I needed to be the exact opposite of the people who brought me up in order to lead an independent life. But that's nonsense."

"Of course. Who else could take over the place anyway?"

"Whatever happens, I'll at least be happy with actually making a decision. To have one thing settled when so much is up in the air."

She didn't ask me outright, but she undoubtedly wanted to know what my plans were, whether I was going to accept the job Helga and Fred had offered me. I didn't think I had much to offer at the hospice—a representative of life where everything was doomed? I had never seen myself as that kind of person, but maybe something in me had changed. The joy of having been able to do this for Mother stifled the anxiety over my imminent loss. We were here because it was possible to hold your head high despite everything, possible to surrender with dignity. When all was said and done Mother and I were not in the hands of professionals, but rather held and supported by friends, and they had changed us. Each breath was impregnated with unrest, finality, and anxiety over what awaited us in the near future, but there was resistance in the void and something tangible to hold on to. I took Helena by the arm and as we walked back up the steps I told her I would think about it. The ceremony was about to begin and people were arriving: Gloria's coworkers, friends of the Cannabis Museum, and the young girl from the reception, her eyes as heavy with makeup as when I first saw her. On the benches closest to the door were a few of Libertas' patients along with Monica, Ljudmila, Helga, and Ramji, and up front close to the first bench Mother and Duncan sat in their wheelchairs, gaunt but with expressions of joy that would have made me cry in the long-gone, hung-over days of summer. The low reggae sounds of the band Satiricon provided a background for the hubbub while Steven took his place by the altar and exchanged Rasta blessings with the vicar. Finally Gloria made her entrance and the nuptials were sealed with a kiss and applause.

"We should also applaud the grand newlyweds over here," Gloria said and asked us to rise. "To Duncan and Eva, who will unfortunately not be able to join us at the party later on."

Mother was in tears over the generosity of the young couple to let dying pensioners share their big day, and said that this more than made up for my absence at her and Duncan's wedding. We headed to Highland with our trusty Ramji at the wheel. He was himself at a turning point in his life; he was going to visit his village, Nainital, for the first time in eleven years, and spend the New Year celebrations with his family.

"Have a safe trip, dear Ramjiminn, and thank you for all your driving," Mother said when they said their good-byes at the door. "Give Buddha my greetings."

Darkness sprawled across in the living room and Mother and Duncan fell asleep in his bed. I helped Helena pack warm clothes and a raincoat for her trip to Kingussie, the childhood haunt of the Knight in the Kilt. She had agreed to take him to the Scottish Highlands and spend Hogmanay with him at a hotel by Loch Laggan. Duncan had dismissed the idea at first, claiming it was silly to embark on a journey when you were as good as dead—what on earth for? But in the end Mother managed to persuade him to go.

"You'll be here when we get back, won't you, Trooper? Promise me?" Helena said when we carried the cases down into the hall and prepared to say good-bye. I had no answer so I just held her tighter, trying to fill the silence with the only certainty I had—that ahead of me lay events that I could neither handle, nor comprehend. "I know you'll be here," she said and repeated. "I know you'll be here when we get back."

And so the days passed until the new year. Mother wrote letters and had a final look at her tapes to make sure nothing was missing. I stayed awake by her side when she slipped into unconsciousness and prepared for the end, either perfectly guileless, or shivering from fathomless misery. We held on for dear life to the only thing that elevated the situation from this bewilderment: to, above all else, follow through with our plan. Maybe it did exist, a million light years from death—the place where people died satisfied and content, happy to shake hands with the Reaper. Maybe it existed for people who where comatose, lost to the world and without thought, people who had disappeared into the darkness; but as long as life was still all that occupied the heart, each breath, and each thought, you didn't want to let go of it. I wondered what it would be like to continue being a part of this, to continue down this path that had helped Mother and I work a bit on the tangles and twists, accept the mistakes that Death left behind and the conflicts his predecessor, Life and its wonders, had brought us. In the end nothing would be explained fully, but at least the silence was not full of gaping wonder.

When I entered the house that last day of the year, Dr. Fred had already set up in the lounge. The camera was on, watching him pour silent death into a glass: 9 grams Pentobarbital, 15 grams Ethanol, 15 grams distilled water, 250 milligrams Saccharine, 11 grams Propylene Glycol, 65 grams syrup, and a drop of Anise oil. Mother had been given three 10-milligram doses of a suppressant since early morning to stop her from vomiting. She was lying in bed watching a Christmas Special on TV. It was *The Lord of the Rings*, a movie she had never understood and found tedious.

"Isn't this that film you were always watching when we lived on Spítala Street?"

"I can't remember," I said. "But then I tended to be hung over a lot on Spítala Street. And then I'd watch TV. Do you remember? How often I was hung over? I think it was your home brew. It made me pretty sick."

"Of course I remember, Trooper, you'd lie in all day watching war movies and eating Danishes. I've never understood all this ruckus myself. How come people enjoy this sort of thing? These disgusting slimy creatures for instance? And all this war nonsense?"

"It's the adventure, right?"

"Maybe, but I have to say that our adventure has been a lot more fun. All these things we did. I was thinking about it earlier, how long ago we set off from Spítala Street. And so much has happened. Just imagine if we'd never have come to Highland . . . or Hotel Europa? How would we have survived this? And all the things we've done. All these interesting and fun things that are down to you, my lovely Trooper. Because it's certainly not down to anyone else, the fun we had. Maybe there's one thing that's not absurd in that war movie of yours, and that's this Frodo fellow, the one with the broad neck—he reminds me a bit of you."

"Oh?"

"Because he has to go through all this trouble with that ring. And it got me thinking: that is how it must have been for my Trooper. My cancer is like those slimy creatures and all the evil of the ring. My Trooper has to carry me through all of this to destroy it. I told Duncan about it and he thought I was quite clever to make the connection. He thought I didn't get the film at all—because I nod off during the battles. But don't you agree, aren't I clever to have realized this with you and Frodo?"

"You've always been clever, Mom . . . though I'm no Frodo."

"Oh, yes you are, Trooper, you are so much more than all these fellows chopping down the slimy creatures. That's what I wanted to tell you, more than anything, my lovely boy, that you have done so well. The greatest hero of them all. You did more than anyone else would have done. And you forgave everything, everything I did. Even though I yelled at you. You did it all for me, my Trooper, you helped me more than anyone."

That was the moment I started crying, and Mother cried too and leaned against me. We sat there for the longest time, holding each other, crying together in the living room in Highland, by the window where the moon glowed in the sky and pulled at the waves by the Dutch coast, in time with the waves breaking in Iceland, clawing our old country back into the sea, like the hearts quaking in our chests.

"This is best way," she whispered. "To do it while we're alone here. I told Duncan I would do it while he was away so it would just be you here with me, my super trooper. I want it now before the Morphine wears off or takes me into oblivion. I want to do it while I'm still conscious. While you're here with me."

I took her into my arms and carried her across the living room, down the hall to the nook where the clock resonated steadily into the future, further into time where the doctor sat silent in the corner and kept to himself. It was just the two of us, my mother and I, two people beyond everything that had happened and everything that would never be forgotten.

"This way is right, my Trooper. It was all right from the very start."

I lay her down on the bed and put the bottle in her hand. It was sherry on Spítala Street, stars sparkled over Highland in the frosty night and the shimmer of her breath flew in between everything as I sat there crying with her in my arms and the last day was done.

Sölvi Björn Sigurðsson is the author of three books of poetry, as well as three novels. Most recently, *The Icelandic Water Book* was published in the fall of 2013. A translator of classical poetry, he has also received distinguished nominations for his translation of Rimbaud's *A Season in Hell*. His *Diabolical Comedy*, a modern take on *The Divine Comedy*, has been translated into Finnish, Swedish, and Danish.

Helga Soffía Einarsdóttir grew up in Tanzania, and has since lived in Copenhagen, Barcelona, and Edinburgh. She has an MA in Translation Studies from the University of Iceland and has worked as a freelance translator and proofreader. Her translations (into Icelandic), include works by Zadie Smith, Alexander McCall Smith, and Lemony Snicket.

DATE DUE

Open Letter—the University of Rochester's nonprofit, literary translation press—is one of only a handful of publishing houses dedicated to increasing access to world literature for English readers. Publishing ten titles in translation each year, Open Letter searches for works that are extraordinary and influential, works that we hope will become the classics of tomorrow.

Making world literature available in English is crucial to opening our cultural borders, and its availability plays a vital role in maintaining a healthy and vibrant book culture. Open Letter strives to cultivate an audience for these works by helping readers discover imaginative, stunning works of fiction and poetry, and by creating a constellation of international writing that is engaging, stimulating, and enduring.

Current and forthcoming titles from Open Letter include works from Argentina, Bulgaria, France, Greece, Latvia, Poland, South Africa, and many other countries.

www.openletterbooks.org